COLORS OF DEATH

Fifteen Tales of Horror

RONA VASELAAR

Thought Catalog Books
Brooklyn, NY

THOUGHT CATALOG BOOKS

Copyright © 2015 by Rona Vaselaar

First edition, 2015
ISBN 978-1518738593
10 9 8 7 6 5 4 3 2 1

Founded in 2010, Thought Catalog is a website and imprint dedicated to your ideas and stories. We publish fiction and non-fiction from emerging and established writers across all genres.

Cover photography by © Christopher Campbell

*Dedicated to my mother, who taught me to read
and, by extension, how to write*

CONTENTS

CHAPTER 1.

COMING HOME FOR DINNER

PART ONE: ANDREW

The best and worst days of my life were separated by two years, three months, four days, three hours, and seven minutes, give or take a few seconds.

The best? The day of my wedding. It was that moment where my eyes swept along the curve of my wife's white gown and up to the tears in her eyes, watching them pour down as I said, "I do." My whole life seemed to culminate in that one perfect moment on that one perfect day.

The worst? The day I lost her, sitting in the ER, watching the surgeon come out only twenty minutes after she'd been rushed in. I knew then that she was gone. I had a drunk driver to thank for that.

Maybe it sounds strange, becoming that attached to someone. I married young, I could always find someone else, right? Except that there was no one else. When I met her, it was like something inside me clicked into place. Everywhere we went, she bled color into the world, filling my vision with a kind of beauty that I can't express, no matter how many useless words fill this page. She was my one and my only.

Jessica. Sorry, it's still hard to even write her name. It feels like the weight on my chest gets heavier every time.

After her death, I went into a deep depression, as is to be expected. I stopped eating and going outside. I practically lived on the couch because I couldn't bear to be in our bed. I had her favorite pink silk nightgown perpetually balled up in my fist. It was like I could hold on to that one piece of her forever.

Things went on like this for months, even after my family tried to intervene. I just couldn't move on. I wouldn't let anyone touch her things. I still DVRed her favorite shows. I would make her favorite foods and then leave them on the counter, never touching them for myself.

I was a mess.

But time goes on. And life goes on, whether you want it to or not. Whether it's fair or not. I started with her toothbrush. One day I caught myself staring at it for over an hour. And then, on an impulse, I grabbed it and threw it in the trashcan. I sobbed for about twenty minutes after. It's like a spell was broken. I gradually went back to daily life.

Nothing was ever the same, and grief never disappears, you just learn to experience it differently. I had moved on as much as I ever would.

Five years, two months, twelve days, four hours, and two minutes after the moment I lost her, I got her back.

I'm an editor for our local newspaper, not too bad a job. She would be proud of me. But sometimes I get back late at night. This happened to be one of those nights.

I trudged in at 11:45, thinking that I'd grab a beer since I'd been particularly productive that day and, hell, I deserved one. Her voice wafted to me from the kitchen.

"Hi, honey, you're back so late!"

Her soft, sweet voice froze me in place.

After she'd passed, I'd often have dreams where she was still alive. She'd convince me that everything that had passed had been nothing but a misunderstanding, and I'd always end up believing her. I'd hold her in my arms and just as I was about to kiss her, I'd wake up on that grungy couch, tears already starting to form in my eyes as reality sunk back in all too quickly.

I figured I was having another one of those dreams.

I squatted down and tried to steady my breathing. It had helped with my panic attacks in the past, maybe it would help me stay calm now. I inhaled and exhaled slowly, trying to will myself to wake up.

And then she popped around the corner.

She looked just like the day she had left for work when the accident happened. Her blonde hair was wavy with just one piece of her bangs longer than the others. Her blue eyes practically jumped out of her skull, they were so big. She was tall and slender, dressed in a simple black dress and a dress coat.

Now I knew I was dreaming. It was like she'd jumped right out of my nightmares.

"What are you doing down there? Come on, I've tried to keep dinner warm for you!"

"YOU'RE NOT REAL!" I screamed. It was more to convince myself than anything else.

In a moment, she was at my side. "Andrew, what happened? What's wrong?" I could feel her eyes searching my face, so I hid it behind my trembling hands. This was bad. I was having a breakdown.

I tried to ward her off again. "GO AWAY, LEAVE ME ALONE!"

This time, she put her arms around me. Her lilac perfume washed through my insides, staining my heart. This was her. This was her touch. I could feel it down to my bones that it was her.

"It's ok, it's ok, shh. Everything is ok, just relax..."

All the resistance I'd had fell away at that point. I cried in her arms for hours. I wouldn't let her go. I knew I was dreaming, but maybe this time I could make it last. Maybe I could just dream forever and never wake up. I was realizing now just how much I wanted that.

Jessica eventually led me to our room. I refused to let go of her, so she climbed into bed with me, snuggling into my arms just like she used to. I tried to remain awake, knowing that once I fell asleep in my dream it was all over. I stared at her perfect face, trying to etch it into my memory. In the end, all my strength drained away and I fell into a deep sleep.

I woke up the next morning, steeling myself for a long day. Maybe I'd call into work sick. Or would it be better to go in? Maybe I shouldn't be alone.

I was contemplating these questions when I opened my eyes and saw that Jessica was still there.

I was speechless, staring at her sleeping form until her eyes fluttered open.

"Hey." Her coarse morning voice, just like I'd remembered. "You're up early. Are you ok? Do you feel better?" She rubbed the sleep out of her eyes, just like I'd remembered. Her every movement... just like I'd remembered.

It felt like all the prayers I'd ever prayed had come true at that moment. So maybe I was still dreaming... maybe I really could dream forever.

I called into work sick and I spent the day with Jessica. It was like she'd never left. She cooked me breakfast. We lazed around the couch and watched stupid romantic comedies. We kissed over and over again. That whole day I wouldn't let go of her. She was always in my arms. She was mine again.

And then, that night, we made love.

That was the moment that convinced me I wasn't in a dream. This was real, it was tangible, it was intimate, it was everything it should have been and more. I knew now I was in the real world with my real wife.

I can honestly say I'd never been happier. I took a full week off of work and just spent time with her. It was the best gift I'd ever been given. Gradually, the past five years began to feel like some bad joke. Here was my wife, and she'd never even left.

Of course, I noticed some things were off. We never left the house. With her home, it seemed natural for us to stay in together. I saw our kitchen stocked with food, even though neither of us had gone to the store.

She never told anyone else that she was back. I never told them, either. It wasn't that I was keeping her a secret. The moment she came back into my life, it was like the rest of the world didn't exist, like it had never existed in the first place.

Lastly, we never addressed her death. I was petrified of bringing it up, as though it would break the delicate balance of her reappearance and she'd be gone again. I just pretended she had never gone, and gradually began to believe it myself.

After a week, I was sufficiently assured that she wasn't going anywhere. I went back to work. I'd come home to a home-cooked meal and romantic evenings. The spring came back into my step and I was always whistling, much to the annoyance of other subway passengers.

It was bliss.

Then it shattered.

The burglar broke in around one in the morning. He was an amateur, unable to jimmy the lock. He thought he could break the downstairs window and we wouldn't hear. Fucking idiot. I jumped to my feet, Jessica following close behind as I rushed down the stairs. I'd grabbed a baseball bat I keep in my room, but of course the moron had a gun.

I was protecting Jessica as best I could, shielding her and trying to hold down my panic. If I died now, I'd be separated from her again. My heart was thumping wildly.

The guy's face – seriously, not even a ski mask? – changed abruptly as he stared at Jessica. It was a look of sheer terror. I've never seen someone that scared.

"Oh, fuck, what the fuck, you sick bastard, what the fuck is wrong with her?!"

That was probably one of the most confusing moments of my life, second only to my dead wife cooking me dinner.

He practically jumped out the window as I turned back to face Jessica.

You know, when Jessica died, I didn't really have a chance to look at her. She was gone before I could see what the car accident had done to her. And, of course, there was no open casket visitation.

Now, however, I had the opportunity to see clearly for myself. I could see the bruising descending diagonally from her left shoulder down, matching the seatbelt that she'd been thrown against at 70 miles an hour. Her face was smashed in, chunks of glass jutting out from where the windshield had been crushed into her head. There was a piece of glass stuck in her right eye, a mess of puss and blood painting her face. Her right arm was twisted at all the wrong angles. You could tell she'd tried to get it in front of her face in time to lessen the blow. The rest of her was black and blue and a mess of blood.

"Should we call the cops?"

Her voice took me out of my daze. This was surreal. She looked at me innocently, as though she was unaware of the mess that her body was in.

After that, I tried everything I could to fix her. I washed her up and removed all the chunks of glass, but the moment I turned my back to throw them in the trash they reappeared. Blood flowed from her cuts in endless streams, converging into a river of gore that swelled at her feet. Although she continued to cook and clean for me and even come into our bed, there was nothing I could do to help her.

As time went on, her body started to decay. I could tell it was happening when she began to swell up, her stomach distending and her skin turning a sickly shade of yellow. The smell came next. It was obvious she was trying to cover it up with perfume. I watched as her hair began to fall away and her skin started to rot.

After a month or so, I realized there was no way we could continue like this. So I sat Jessica down.

"Honey, I want you to know that I love you very much... But we both know that you shouldn't be here. Please, I need to know... what happened to you?"

Until I reached the end of my question, Jessica held that perfect, innocent smile. But as soon as I finished, she broke down and began sobbing, puss pouring out of her eyes instead of tears.

"I know this might make you hate me, but... I made a deal."

My heart sank. "Jessica, what did you do?"

She sniffled. "Death isn't anything like what people say. He looked like an ordinary man to me. And when I died, it wasn't so bad, just like drifting through nothingness. But I could still see you sometimes. Sometimes I'd find myself standing next to you, watching you. And I could feel your pain. I wanted so much to help you.

"So I asked Death to let me come back. Just one more chance. For a long time, he wouldn't listen. It's against the laws of nature, he said. It's not my place, not anymore. But...

"But then he saw your lifespan was shortening. You were supposed to live to be an old man, you were supposed to have kids and a full life... but instead, your life was getting shorter and shorter by the minute, like a candle about to burn out. It went from 80 years to 70, to 60, to 50, to 40...

"That's when he made the deal with me. He knew that if I came back, your lifespan would return to normal. He told me that our bond was too strong, we couldn't be separated, it was a mistake to pull us apart in the first place. He told me I could come back.

"The thing is, though, I couldn't let anyone but you see me or have any contact with me. If I did, I would have to die again. Dead people don't belong in this world, but I wanted to be with you, no matter what the cost."

At this point, Jessica was in hysterics. I did my best to comfort her, my soothing hand careful not to pull away her rotting skin. I spoke in a low, soft voice until she gradually relaxed. She cried herself to sleep and I placed her in our bed.

I'm writing this because I want someone, anyone, to know what I know now. Sometimes, love hurts. Sometimes it hurts the ones you love the most. My love for Jessica became her burden, and now she is rotting here in front of my eyes. I can see how painful it is for her. I can see that balance must be restored.

I've still got my dad's old glock in the gun safe downstairs. In a moment I'll lay down next to the woman I love more than anything in the world and I'll restore the balance. At least this time we can go together.

PART TWO: JESSICA

I know that Andrew had all the best intentions, he really did. That's one of the things I love about him: he is genuinely a good-hearted person.

The bullet entering my skull was definitely more painful than the car accident. Yes, I can still feel pain. And, if I'm being honest, it's the worst pain I've ever felt. Just think of it: you get shot in the head, but instead of a "bang" and then darkness, you simply can't die. And because you're a corpse, your body can't heal.

When I felt that pain, it stunned me. I didn't even scream, not at first. Can a corpse still go into shock? Apparently so, because I remained in an excruciating stillness until I heard the gun go off again.

In the end, I'm the one who did this to Andrew. It was my selfish wish.

I met him when I was in college. To be honest, I never intended to get married. I grew up watching my mother and father flounder around, trapped in their own loveless marriage. Maybe they had loved each other once upon a time, but even I could see that, by the time they had me, my father couldn't have cared less if my mother lived or died. I guess I just grew up not believing in love.

Andrew and I took a Gender Studies class together in college, believe it or not. We were both a little on the shy side and sat next to each other at the back of the class. We often paired up for group projects. I was stunned to see how hard he worked. He did every reading, even the suggested readings that no one else bothered with.

I asked him why once. When I did, I saw his eyes sparkle for the first time. "My passion is writing. I want to write the most realistic characters and relationships possible. I'll take any class that I think can help."

That sparkle jump-started my heart and I fell in love with him right there.

You know, Andrew and I knew almost everything about each other. But I bet he didn't know that was the moment when I fell in love. I bet he didn't know how his eyes magnetize when he's talking about his writing.

He also didn't know that I read everything he'd ever written. Every paper, every short story, every article for our crappy school newspaper... when we were married, his mom handed me all of his writings that she'd collected over the years. Did you know he started when he was four? I read every single one. I could never get enough. Every word brought me a little closer to him.

He didn't know that every morning before I went to work I would kiss him on the forehead, just in case something happened and I didn't get to see him that evening. I did it on the morning of the accident, too.

And he didn't know the most important part of the deal I made with Death.

Dying itself wasn't painful. You know what was painful? Watching Andrew suffer, with me not being able to do anything. I could only watch. I watched him pray to gods I know he didn't believe in just to see me one more time. I saw him staring at the kitchen knives we bought together, imagining slicing his own skin open. I saw him crying over the pink silk nightgown that I had bought for our honeymoon.

Those moments were even more painful that this corpse-like existence.

That's why I made the deal. That's why I did what I did. I thought I was helping him. I didn't understand what kind of burden I was giving him.

When I came back it was bliss. Sure, the first night was hard. I know that my sudden appearance did a number on him. I know that he was confused and scared. But I thought it didn't matter. Because now we were together and now we could be happy... And we were happy, for longer than I deserved.

Why did I follow him downstairs that night? It's a good question, and I'm sorry that I don't have a better answer. In that one moment of adrenaline and fear, looking at Andrew and knowing how vulnerable and fragile his life was, I forgot Death's conditions. Andrew jumped out of the room and I went wild, everything in my mind and heart going blank, except for Andrew's face.

And, as you already know, everything fell apart.

I didn't know that Andrew could tell how much pain I was in. Living in this decaying body hasn't been easy. I didn't know that Andrew loved me so much that he would so gladly go into the afterlife with me.

And I didn't know that he thought I'd be able to go with him.

The deal was that I'd return to the realm of the living to live out the rest of Andrew's natural life. He was supposed to die when he was 82 years old. Either way, I have to live those remaining years.

With or without him.

It was hard, burying him with my muscles quickly decaying. I'm not as strong as I used to be, but I couldn't bear the thought of his family finding him like this... better for them to think that he up and disappeared. Maybe I can write a letter convincing enough to give them some semblance of peace.

I only have one good eye and that's slowly collapsing in my skull. Writing this has been a challenge. I'm glad this confession is almost over.

As for me, I don't know where I'll go. I have to leave because if my body is found here, God knows what everyone will think of Andrew. I don't want him or his reputation to suffer any more for me.

As I lose my mobility, I've begun to realize just what this deal means. There will soon come a time when I won't be able to move, speak, see, feel... I'll be bound to a skeleton, left alone somewhere far away from the house that catalogued our pain and sorrow, or lives and our deaths. I thought about burying myself with Andrew, but there was simply no way to do it.

I'm trying not to be afraid, but it's so hard to conceive of those hours of darkness and loneliness, unbroken until his time runs out. All alone without my Andrew.

Fifty-one years, six months, seven days, two hours, and eleven minutes left to go.

had said 11 pm, but what if they were wrong? What if I had misunderstood? If there was even the slightest chance that the subway was still open, I'd go and take it. If not, hopefully I would be in a good spot to catch a cab.

As I approached the subway station, I saw promising fluorescent lights glowing from its depths. Oh, thank God, I thought to myself. No more worrying about being ripped off, dropped off at the wrong place, or murdered (I've always been a bit paranoid).

I bounded down the stairs, my footsteps echoing and bouncing off the tiled walls. It was pretty empty, but that's what I'd expect so late at night. I walked brusquely to the security check, my spirits lifting immensely. I couldn't wait to get home and shower.

I looked at the guards and stopped in my tracks.

A serious looking Chinese man stared back at me. Rather than the black military-style uniform that I was accustomed to seeing, he was attired in a long cloak with a high collar, very classical Chinese. A strange red and black hat adorned his thick, braided hair. The most troubling aspect of his dress, however, was a thick, yellowing scroll of paper that seemed pasted on to his chest with thick, black Chinese characters scrawled down the front. I tried half-heartedly to read the characters, but they swirled across my line of vision in a confusion of strokes that led me to believe that they must be traditional Chinese.

His piercing eyes ripped through me, freezing my heart to a dead stop.

"Um... hi?"

He continued to stare at me with no answer.

I tried again, in Chinese this time. "Hey, is the subway open? When does it close?"

He stared at me again, his lips set in a straight line. Wow. So helpful.

I was beginning to get extremely uncomfortable. Should I... leave?

I was about to turn around and high-tail it out of there when his lips parted slightly. His eyes remained fixed and rigid while his mouth squirmed against his pale skin like a twisting worm. But, no matter how long I waited, no sound came out.

Once he had finished... speaking?... He looked at me expectantly.

If I had been in America, I would have taken him for a lunatic and turned tail. But, the thing is, I was in Beijing. Maybe this was just a part of the culture I didn't understand. Maybe something weird was happening and I didn't quite get it. Maybe it was only weird to me but not to your average Beijinger.

So, stupid as I was, I didn't let it end there.

Maintaining strong eye contact, I pointed to myself, then pointed to the stairs that led into the subway.

He gave a slight, almost imperceptible nod and I passed through without further issue.

Next came the turnstiles. I tried to swipe my handy-dandy subway card, but nothing registered. They were open anyway, and the guard wasn't paying me any attention, so I stepped through with a shrug. Well, whatever, free ride for me.

As I descended into the harsh light of the tunnel, I began berating myself for making this journey. Why didn't I just stay in the dorm with my friends? Well, actually, the answer to that question was pretty simple: who wanted to sleep on a rock-hard bed with a bunch of drunks? No, thanks, I'll take my chances with Creepy Subway Guard.

To my surprise, a plethora of people awaited me when I arrived at my platform. At least, I think it was my platform. It was situated where my platform was supposed to be, but the signs had... changed? Instead of the chic plastic that slicked the walls in the morning, there were heavy wood signs with carved squiggles that I couldn't decipher.

I began to grow colder as I wondered what the hell I had gotten myself into.

However, I managed to stay calm due to the crowd. If there were this many people waiting for the train, then it had to arrive and go somewhere, right? I needed to remain calm. Just... think of this as an adventure. Like I'm Bilbo Baggins or something.

It took me a moment to realize that something else was wrong. Everyone was silent.

Usually the subway was a cacophony of laughter, idle chatter, and angry voices pushing their way through the crowds. On this occasion, however, the silence was so palpable I could taste it, like sawdust on my tongue.

And when I looked around, their mouths were all moving. Just as the guard before, their lips blossomed and closed like dragonsnaps, but no sound came forth.

I'll admit it, I was just about to walk back up those stairs and leave when the subway pulled up to the platform.

All of a sudden, the still passengers burst to life and filled the thus-far empty train. I was swept along with them, practically carried into the train car by a mob of businessmen, old women, and children.

Wait, children?

I looked down and saw a six-year-old girl at my feet, her eyes solemn and her hair pulled back into pigtails. She appeared to be accompanied by no one and none of the other passengers paid any attention to her.

I knelt down to her eye level. "Hey, there. Do you know where your mommy and daddy are?"

I should have kept my mouth shut. Curse my American meddling.

Without blinking, her eyes as cold and blank as chalk, her mouth shuddered and twisted.

No sound.

Fuck fuck FUCK.

Suddenly, I was approached by another passenger.

By this point, all eyes were on me. I was used to being stared at because my porcelain skin so clearly marks me as a foreigner, but this was somehow different. Their stares were intense rather than curious. For the first time I really felt like I didn't belong.

The passenger who approached me was a man perhaps in his late 50s, with graying hair and a scraggly mustache to match. He kept his mouth pressed in a firm line as he handed me a block of chocolate.

What?

He placed it in my hand, stared right at my gaping jaw, and waited patiently. The other passengers continued staring. Their stares got more intense, if that's even possible. But the mouths, they continued their hell-dance uninterrupted. I shuddered.

I don't know why I did what I did next. It was stupid and horrible and it probably saved my life.

I bit into the brick of chocolate. Immediately an awful taste filled my mouth and I began to choke, spitting the mush out onto the ground without hesitation. One thought surfaced through the murky confusion in my mind: mud.

"What the fuck is this? Is this some kind of a jo-"

And then, all of a sudden, a roar of noise filled the air. I could hear hundreds of conversations issuing from those grimy lips, accompanied by appropriate laughter, snorts, scoffs, and coughs. All eyes were still on me, but for all intents and purposes it sounded like a regular Beijing subway.

The shock must have registered on my face because the man who had approached me laughed. "I think you're lost."

I stared at him. "N... No. I'm going to Haidian Huangzhuang station."

A chorus of laughter rang out around him.

"Do you know where this train goes?"

Now I was getting frustrated. "Haidian Huangzhuang! I ride it every morning!"

He nodded sagely. "Yes, and I'm sure in the morning it DOES go to Haidian. But at night, at night it serves a different purpose." I struggled to keep up with his muddled Beijing accent. What was he saying?

"Listen carefully."

Obediently, I tuned into the conversation next to me. It was between a young man, no more than 20 years old, and a middle-aged woman wearing a red scarf.

"What happened to you?" asked the man.

"Car accident. You?"

He blushed. "Suicide."

She hit his shoulder with a scoff of disgust. "You should have valued your life more! Now what will happen when you are judged, hm?"

The man looked agitated and preoccupied with his thoughts. In the mean time, I had turned ashen.

I looked back at the man.

"Where… does this train go?"

"Where? I think you already know."

I began to panic as the train ground to a halt.

"And this is your stop."

My panic grew. "No… no, I don't want to go!"

He smiled at me kindly. "Trust me, you'll be fine."

As the doors slid open, he shoved me out.

I found myself alone, standing in the bright fluorescent lights of a subway platform identical to the Tuanjiehu station. For one moment only I looked around, waiting breathlessly for a sign of life. Then I bolted up the stairs.

As I ran past the security guard, I heard his laughter call after me. It bounced sickeningly off the walls and wormed its way into my skull. I shrieked and sprinted out of the station, desperate to escape that sound.

Suddenly, I was standing on Sanlitun again, as though I had never left. The street was congested with people who seemed completely indifferent to the fact that I had almost been sent to the underworld. They chattered by while I whirled back around.

The subway was dark, deserted, and locked.

I trembled quietly as I stared into that abyss. Now I knew what the inside of that darkness looked like.

A young Chinese couple approached me. The man stuttered out in broken English, "Are you ok? You look sick."

I stared at him, thinking vaguely of the young suicide victim, on his way to judgment. "I want to go home," I muttered in Chinese, casting a sidelong glance back at the subway.

his hands were cut off, hands that presumably once touched underage children; his eyes were cut out so they could never view child porn again; and, just for good measure, his penis had been hacked off, for reasons that should be obvious.

This was how The Judge introduced himself to the town.

The Judge is the name the papers would eventually give him. Or her. Although the papers mourned the gruesome sight being displayed right next to the community park's playground (where no doubt Mel had been lurking the night before), they weren't overly concerned with the pedophile having his livelihood cut short (quite literally). Of course, there were those who demanded answers, but most people were quite content to let the matter slide. As far as they were concerned, The Judge was just taking out the trash.

The Judge visited again just two weeks later.

April 28th, the back alley of Silverfox Bar. Veronica Jeffers, aged 28, had her tongue sliced out for falsely accusing a man of raping her. She'd been hoping to swindle money out of the deal, but she hadn't thought through her lie very well and, fortunately, the man was set free. Unfortunately, Veronica wasn't prosecuted. Veronica's fate was somewhat more merciful than Mel's: before anyone found her, she had already drowned in her own blood. The stiffness was already setting in her muscles by the time the ambulance arrived.

The media made the connection right away, and thus The Judge was named and tagged. He'd scour our neighborhood streets for filth and scum, keeping our little community safe and sound. He was obviously a very controversial figure: some hailed him for his bravery, some hoped he would meet the same fate as his victims.

But everybody was interested in him.

A few more deaths popped up in the weeks that followed. A pair of parents who had disowned their fourteen-year-old daughter for being gay was found victim of two crudely performed lobotomies. A relatively inconspicuous man was gutted down by the creek: authorities found an array of missing neighborhood pets in his basement, all tortured and dismembered.

Our neighborhood seemed to sparkle just a little brighter with each death. There was, however, one problem that we did not account for.

You see, our little neighborhood is only a few thousand people. How many child-molesting, animal-torturing, prejudiced scumbags can live in such a small area? It was bound to happen sooner or later, but in our case it was sooner: The Judge simply ran out of people to hunt.

A few weeks went by without (bloody and gruesome) incident. Most people believed that The Judge had retired from his short-lived career, having cleaned the neighborhood and kept the streets safe.

But on May 30th, around 5 pm, a young child named Barbara Tib was found on Lakeview Road, severely beaten with her lips sewn shut. She was about nine years old.

The neighborhood was in an uproar of shock and bewilderment. Could this be the work of The Judge? If so, why would The Judge hurt a child?

The answer became apparent with a little prodding from Barbara's schoolmates: Barbara was a notorious bully, one whose actions were often ignored by the teachers and playground monitors. She'd been beaten just as she'd beaten the weaker girls. Her lips had been sealed so she couldn't hurl her hateful insults ever again.

At this point, it was too late to stop it. And it became increasingly worse.

Barbara's parents were the next to go, beaten to death for failing to discipline their own child. The teachers who had stood idly by as she bullied the other children were tied up and thrown in the river to drown, their struggles ignored by the rest of the world.

A few days later, Jenna Tanson, who had once caused a fender bender by texting and driving, was run down with a car. She was nineteen.

The police were frantic looking for this man. The rest of us were slowly giving in to panic. We had encouraged The Judge at first, but now we had to wonder: by what standards was he now judging us?

Things have gotten much worse in the last week. A woman caught littering has disappeared – I wonder if she'll ever turn up. The kid next door who occasionally smokes a little weed had so much heroin forcibly injected into his system that he OD'd.

As for me, I've stopped going out of doors. I follow the news updates but I keep my windows nailed shut and a gun beside my bed at all times. My neighbors are slowly disappearing. And now, I have to ask myself:

What might I have done wrong?

CHAPTER 4.

MY OLDER SISTER

My life has been average at most.

I lived in a family of two girls and one boy. There was my older sister, Jenny, me, and my younger brother, Alex. We had a typical childhood, I guess. Jenny was popular, with her blonde hair, blue eyes, and skinny frame. Alex early on showed a penchant for sports and became the star athlete of the family. But I, just like the rest of my life, was very... average.

I wasn't overly smart. I wasn't ugly but I didn't stand out. I had a small group of friends.

I was average.

But I idolized my older sister.

Jenny was everything I would never be. She had friends upon friends upon friends. She had a string of boyfriends starting from the time she was 11. There was always some boy, some drama. She grew tired of it, but I loved it.

And Jenny loved me, too. We were really close as children. Mom and dad loved me, sure, but they didn't notice me like they did Jenny and Alex. Because there was nothing special about me, not really. But Jenny didn't see it that way. See, she paid attention to me. She gave me makeovers and taught me about makeup. She used to take me shopping with her popular friends and show me the best clothes to wear for my body shape. She would tell me all about her amazing, glittering life and she would listen if and when I found some small contribution to make to our conversations.

She was my role model.

But sometimes life isn't average. Sometimes it isn't typical. When Jenny was 16 and I was 13, she was found in her room, a bottle of pills spilled out next to her. I don't think they even bothered with much of an investigation. It was clear what she'd done, although no one really knew why. Life can be funny that way. Sometimes it's the ones who seem happy who are struggling the most.

It was a very difficult time for my family.

But life went on. And as I grew older, I grew to love my average life. My parents paid a little more attention to me, what with Jenny gone. I went to a state university for journalism where I met my husband, Alan. We got married right out of college. I worked for the local paper and he had an office job at a company just a few blocks down the road. Our life was blissful, beautiful, and unremarkable.

Until, that is, I became pregnant.

It started when I was about two weeks late. I've always been as regular as a clock, but at the time work was pretty hectic and I wasn't really paying attention.

And then, one night, I had a terribly real, terribly strange dream.

In the dream, I was in my old childhood room, sitting on the flower-patterned comforter on my twin-sized bed, playing with a pacifier for God knows what reason. In walked Jenny. She came and climbed on the bed. She was toying with an empty pill bottle. And she looked into my eyes.

I don't know why, but I woke up screaming. To be honest, I hadn't paid much thought to Jenny in years, and I'd never had a dream like that. My husband woke up to comfort me, but I was already on my way to the bathroom. I projectile vomited into the toilet for about twenty minutes, thinking of missed periods and pill bottles and Jenny.

I took a pregnancy test that day. It came out positive.

My husband and I were overjoyed. We celebrated with a nice dinner at Havana's on Main. We called our parents, who were both incredibly excited. We talked about baby names and a nursery and all the things you associate with children. We got to bed late, exhausted but happy, cuddling together like newlyweds, dreaming of little cherubs dancing in our arms.

I woke up to see my sister standing next to the bed.

If the night before had been frightening, you can't imagine how this felt. Here she was, Jenny, the real (not so) live Jenny. She stared down at me. I reached out. I almost felt as though I could touch her. But she turned and walked out of the room.

From that day on, Jenny was always there.

She was standing next to the bed when I woke up in the morning. She followed me to work. She watched as I picked out baby clothes, occasionally fingering one or two items that she particularly liked.

She was always there.

Sure, I thought about telling my husband. But what would I say? That his average wife was about to disturb his average life with her newfound ability to see the dead? Unlikely. Rather, I considered it a strange and

and I figured what we were going to do with it. No harm in that, anyway.

The first few days, I ghosted up and down the wide hallways, my hands trailing lightly along the walls, wondering if Phillip had touched them this way, too. I wandered in and out of rooms, taking note of the things Phillip had brought from our old home, the things he had bought himself, the things I had given him. I didn't touch any of that. I knew I would have to one day, but for now neither my mother nor I had the heart to move any of it.

I moved into a guest bedroom and left everything else perfectly in place.

Some parts of the house Phillip clearly never used. The basement, for one. For such a nice house, the basement was surprisingly bare, with its expanse of decrepit walls and discolored floors. I didn't bother stalking through the endless hallways down there. If Phillip hadn't been there, then there was no meaning. The attic, too, was surprisingly empty, despite being the perfect place for storage. There were a few rooms here and there that were left alone.

Phillip never really got settled in the house he dreamt of calling a home.

While I lived there, it was like living in limbo. Everything seemed ready for the day that Phillip would come back... it felt like I was waiting for him, too.

But I still wasn't prepared for it when it happened.

I came home from work one day, utterly exhausted. I hadn't really been sleeping lately. Every time I came close to sleep, visions of my brother's dangling body would pop into my head and I'd hear the creaking sound of the rope swinging under his weight. No good, I'd rather stay awake.

I got home and trudged up the stairs to the guest bathroom. I stared at the mirror for a few minutes in mute silence, memorizing every aspect of it. The gold gilt frame, the small chip on the left side, and the words "DID YOU MISS ME?" scrawled across the front in red lipstick.

My vision swam and I stumbled out towards my bed. Was my lack of sleep giving me hallucinations? Was I dreaming right now? Could be, all I'd had lately were nightmares, if I'd been able to sleep at all. Maybe this was all one big nightmare.

A few minutes of willing myself to wake up and the ensuing frustrated tears proved that no, it was not a dream. It was very real. Too real.

Even so, I dragged myself into my bed. I'd held off sleep as long as I could, I'd reached my limit. Everything felt fuzzy and strange. My brain barely made sense of the situation, which is probably why I was so calm.

I passed out for thirteen hours. Thirteen long, torturous hours. Thirteen hours of that swaying body, that creaking, and nothing else.

When I woke up, the message was gone. All part of my fatigued brain. Either that or some cruel trick of nature. Perhaps both? It didn't matter, it was gone now.

Things were normal for a few days. My resolve weakened and I gave in to sleep, as horrible as my dreams were. They drained my spirit and left me lifeless, a body without a soul, wandering through a life that was no longer my own.

A week later, I received another message.

This one was a post-it note stuck to the fridge in the first-floor kitchen.

"MILK EGGS SUGAR LIPSTICK – P"

I couldn't explain this away, no matter how hard I tried. I picked the paper up and held it between my fingers, running my fingertips across the messy script. Phillip's handwriting only got this messy when he was really on a roll, trying to push the story out of the pen before it dissolved away in his brain. It was almost as though he'd scrawled off the note during one of his "sessions" – that's what he used to call it when he got really into a story, so far into it that he couldn't see reality anymore.

I walked through the house, clutching that note like it could save my life, like it could save Phillip's. After I'd exhausted myself, I fell asleep with the note balled up in my fist.

I woke up a few hours later to the sound of music.

It was floating up from the downstairs. Queen, my brother's favorite. He'd put it on every night when he studied. It drove my mom crazy. I'd learned to live with it. I let the music guide me to the living room where my brother's iPod was plugged into the stereo. I had walked through this house hundreds of times, memorizing every single inch of my brother's life and I knew for a fact that this iPod had never been plugged into this machine. It should have been sitting at his bedside table.

I fell to the ground and held my hands against my head as strains of Somebody to Love pounded into my ears. This couldn't be real, could it? And what if it was? I hadn't asked for this. Of course I wanted my brother back, but I wanted the real him back, not all these little reminders of the man he had been.

I got fired from my job the next week. I'd stopped showing up, opting to sit at home and wait for the next message to appear. Oftentimes there'd be notes on scraps of paper strewn throughout the house. Nothing very important, usually an address here or there, a little "have a nice day, love you!" to someone who had once been special. Sometimes there was more.

It all came to a head one night when I left my computer open for Phillip. It was out of curiosity, really. I wanted to see if he would show up, if he would write something to me. Something especially for me. If we were going to communicate, I wanted it to be direct. Some small part of my mind was still rational, but for the most part I'd abandoned myself to the fantasy of my brother coming out of his coffin.

I woke up to an open word document:

"HI DAVID HI DAVID HI DAVID HI DAviddddddddddd
Did you miss me did you miss me did you miss miss me did miss me did you
I like it here
I likeiit!!!
Come follow me David"

I got really, really drunk that day. I mean really fucking drunk. I didn't know what else to do so I got wasted.

What I was talking to... could it really be Phillip? I didn't think so anymore. If it as Phillip, he wouldn't want to scare me, and this was scaring the fucking shit out of me.

A thought started to seep into my brain, fighting through my drunken haze to make itself heard: maybe this was why Phillip killed himself. There was something... something about this house. Something deep inside, festering, creeping, crawling. It had reached out its slimy claws and taken a hold of Phillip, drew him

graves much like Richard's: old and decrepit. But this headstone was significantly different. It still looked new, with no cracks, moss, or anything else. As I got closer, I realized that it didn't look stone at all.

A few knocks on the side confirmed my suspicions. It was metal. And not only was it metal, but it was hollow on the inside.

I got in touch with the cemetery caretaker, a guy named Andrew Jones. He's been working in the cemetery since the late fifties, a bit after Richard's time, but since Andrew inherited the job from his father, I was hoping he'd have some information on the stone.

"Oh, that old stone? That's an interesting story, Meredith," Andrew said. His gravely voice crackled in over the phone and I had to struggle to hear him. "The guy who bought it, that Stirler, he had a moonshine operation in the twenties during prohibition. But you probably already know that," his laugh cracked like a whip and I found myself wishing he would just get on with the story. "Right, anyway, that's a fake grave. The panels on the side used to open up. Potential buyers would put the money in the headstone. Stirler would come that night and switch it out with his moonshine. The repairs we recorded are from when my father sealed the panels. Prohibition ended and so did Stirler's business, so they weren't needed anymore."

"But didn't anyone notice the headstone? Or was Richard was doing?" I couldn't really fathom that: going more than ten years without a single person noticing the whole operation.

"Oh, sure, everyone in town knew about it. Hell, Stirler's biggest buyer was the sheriff!"

"What?!" My mouth hung slack. This was just the type of drama that I loved finding out about.

"Ayup," Andrew continued, clearly enjoying filling me in on the juicy details. "That's how Stirler managed to stay in business so long. He and the sheriff had an understanding. Sure, the sheriff would arrest him once every few months, but it was just for show. He'd let him out of the tank a few days later and Stirler'd go right back to work. Sure used to drive his wife crazy, though."

"Who, the sheriff's?"

"No, Stirler's..." Suddenly Andrew stopped. "Oh, I guess I'm thinking of someone else. Sorry about that. Forget I said that."

I tried to get more information out of Andrew, but he kept his lips stubbornly sealed. I hung up more confused than ever. None of the newspaper stories ever mentioned Richard having a wife. If he'd been close to any sort of family, it definitely would have been in the obituary.

Luckily, I had an ace up my sleeve. I made the call I'd been thinking about since my trip to the courthouse earlier that day, the call to my "inside connection".

The most valuable tool in conducting research is the elderly. For some cases, they really can't help: if I'm researching something from the mid-1800s, for example. In other cases, they provide valuable eyewitness accounts that no one else can. Unfortunately, a lot of the older people in small towns won't talk about their community's darker history – they feel as though they have to protect the town's reputation by burying the past with their fast-fading bodies. A few of them, however, understand the importance of preserving history as it is, no matter how ugly or frightening.

One such woman is Taalke Klinkenberg. At 94 years old, she's still sharp as a tack and has been filling me in on the darker side of our town's history for the past ten years. Although she's lived in the town her whole life, she's never harbored any warm feelings for its inhabitants. "This town has a lot of sick people in it, Meredith," she once told me. "A lot of sick people and a lot of sick stories. And people shouldn't forget that kind of sickness."

So I called Taalke and we made an appointment for the next day. I headed over to her house – so old and she still lives in that big house down on Fifth Avenue all by herself. I don't know how she does it.

Anyway, as soon as I brought up Richard's name, her eyes started to shine and she leaned forward in her old armchair. That's how I knew this would be a good story.

"Well, now, I was just a baby during Prohibition, but I heard a lot about Richard Stirler once I grew up a little. My father was working in the police department at the time, and, well, I don't mind telling you that he was a regular buyer of Stirler's. But as I got older, I heard him say that something was wrong with that man.

"I'm not surprised that Mr. Jones wouldn't tell you about his wife and child. You see, Richard and Rosemary had been married for just a few years when he bought that property. And after he bought it, he started acting really funny. He was sort of strange to begin with, you know, but after he started making moonshine things got worse. The strain on their relationship was even stronger after Rosemary had her baby boy – Peter, I think they named him. Anyway, about a year after Peter was born – I think that would have been 1933? – Rosemary up and left. Took Peter with her and just walked out overnight.

Richard never heard from her again. He really went south after that. I remember my father talking about it just after Richard killed himself. That was the final straw, he said. Sure, he lived for about ten years after she left him, but he never really recovered. He was sort of a dead man walking. My father used to say that Richard really died in 1933 and wasn't buried until 1936.

"Personally, I always thought it was cruel of Rosemary to leave Richard. When you marry someone, you make a commitment to them, no matter what happens. Richard may have had his problems, but she should have stayed by his side and supported him." She leaned back in her seat, satisfied with her story, and sipped at her coffee. "That's my two cents, anyway," she added as an afterthought. I had a slightly different opinion, but I kept it to myself.

Well, now I had the story, and everything made sense. No mention was made of the wife or child in his obituary because they'd left. Richard had run a moonshine operation and he'd purchased the headstone for business. He killed himself because he could no longer handle the loneliness. No loose ends, no real mystery.

But something didn't feel right.

And I decided to investigate some more.

I wasn't sure where to start until a question came bubbling up in my brain: why would they seal the headstone? Sure, they didn't have a use for it after prohibition, but why take the time and effort to actually seal it? I figured it was to ensure it wasn't used again, or maybe so that local kids wouldn't mess with it, but my curiosity gnawed at me and I decided I was going to check it out for myself.

I decided to go after dark. Cliché, I know, but that way I didn't have to worry about Andrew coming out

Hi, Meredith!

I hope your research is going well. Actually, I am not looking for this information on my own behalf. Richard Stirler would be my great grandfather, I believe? At least, I think that's how he's related. It's been very hard to find information on him. I'm actually doing this for my uncle Peter. He requested any information I could find on him, but I quickly found that my own research skills weren't up for the task!

Could I ask what you've found up to this point?

So glad to hear from you!

Emily

My stomach sank as I read Emily's latest email. Her uncle... Peter? My mind raced back to the little skeleton entombed in the fake gravestone. No. No, no, no. It couldn't be. Peter's a common name, it could be... anyone, right?

I knew there was only one person who could help me at this point.

As soon as I got off work, I drove down to the cemetery. Andrew was outside, stalking through the rows of tombstones, picking up old flowers, trinkets, etc. He didn't even notice me drive in and only became aware of my presence when I was a few rows away. I saw him immediately become nervous.

He was definitely hiding something.

"Andrew, you're not telling me everything you know, are you?"

All semblance of tact went out the window. There was a dead child and I needed to know exactly who it was.

Andrew shifted from one foot to the other and looked down. "Can't say I know what you're talking about, Meredith."

I wanted to yell and scream but I knew better. I understand people. They're not so hard to deal with, and, besides, I'd already planned for this. I pulled a few hundreds out of my wallet and handed them over. "How about we go talk about this in private?"

His eyes widened and I could see him calculating how many bottles of cheap beer this would buy at the local liquor store. He nodded and a few minutes later we found ourselves in his living room, the picture window framing the quiet of the cemetery behind us.

"Meredith, I don't want people in town to know any more about this incident than they have to. I don't know why you're so curious about it, but whatever I tell you stays out of this town. Am I making myself clear?"

I nodded and he continued.

"My father was very good friends with Richard. They used to knock back a couple beers every few nights. That's how Richard got the fake stone set up in the first place – you think he could have done that without my dad's help? Hardly.

"See, Richard made a mistake when he bought that property out on 75. He thought he could make a living as a farmer, but he never really was cut out for that kind of work. Plus, those first few years the crops didn't turn out so well. Not enough rain or sunshine, I think it was. By the time he started up his moonshine operation, he and Rosemary were pretty far in debt.

I knocked hard, all while calling her name. I hoped she was there.

Sure enough, the door cracked open a few moments later. She really did look crazy, staring at me from behind the door chain, glaring daggers into my eyes.

"What do you want?"

I took a deep breath. This was the moment I had been waiting for. "Um... my name is Anna, I live just across town. I read... I read about what happened to your fiancé. And I think you're the only person who can help me. Can you just listen to what I have to say, please?"

I thought for sure I'd get the door slammed in my face. Instead, I was met with a look of surprise, then guilt. A moment later, the chain was off the door and it stood wide open.

"Please, come in."

The house wasn't anything like I'd imagined. It was kept immaculately clean, far from the hoarder's haven I supposed it to be. She led me into a small living room, complete with a sofa and TV. It looked normal enough. On a shelf above the TV I saw a picture of a young man who I assumed to be her late fiancé... I remember thinking he looked a little familiar. His picture must have been included with Esther's story in the newspaper.

We exchanged a few pleasantries and I found that she really did seem normal. She offered me tea and I politely declined. After a few more exchanges, we got to the point.

"Why would you come to me? And how did you find out about my fiancé?"

"Well... it started a few weeks ago. My best friend, Liz, she went missing in the lake out at the national park. I guess she drowned, only... only they can't find her body.

"I was in the library looking for answers and I kept coming across these strange stories. These other people had drowned, but then they came back. And you were one of them. I have to know... what happened to you? Where were you during the time you had disappeared? Please, I need to find Liz."

I could feel tears stinging my eyes. My breath caught in my throat as I tried to remain calm.

Esther looked at me with such pain in her eyes, a pain that I can't describe. It was the pain of a loss that had never healed, a scar that had never stopped throbbing. She glanced out the window, her mind seeming to trail back to an earlier time.

"I have never in all my life told anyone what I am about to tell you. I tell you this because you need to know. Because I don't want you to suffer like I did.

"I was sort of like you when I was your age. Lanky and quiet, but determined and with one hell of an attitude. I thought it was quite the blessing that I was marrying Alan. He never tried to rein me in, always let me run free...

"But that's what ended up getting me into trouble. I went out swimming with some of my friends, despite my parents telling me it wasn't safe. I was a good swimmer, so I wasn't paying attention. The center of the lake is deep, much deeper than it looks..."

Her eyes weren't seeing the same world I was. She'd traveled back through all those years. I was looking at a ghost of a memory.

"I was swimming down when I felt something grab my arm. I tried to wrench myself free, but I couldn't. I struggled until the water filled my lungs and I suffocated with a burning throat. I thought I would die, but that lake... there's something wrong with that lake.

"I didn't die. Instead, I found myself trapped below the water. I saw someone swimming up and away from me, but I couldn't follow them. I couldn't feel my body anymore. I could only feel the water, rushing through me, scattering me like ashes and dust.

"I went on like that for a week. Do you know what it's like, living without a body? Living without being alive? It was torture. I swirled along the bottom of the lake, desperate for any way out.

"And then, someone else came into the water."

She was full-out crying, now, and she rushed on as though she had forgotten me.

"I wish it had been anyone but Alan. Living that kind of existence, do you know what it does to you? I just wanted to escape. I would do anything. I couldn't even stop myself. I could feel myself reaching through the water, reaching with a hand that hadn't been there since I'd drowned. I grasped his leg, even as he searched for me. I grasped him and I didn't let go..."

She wept for a few minutes, utterly incapable of continuing. I shivered in my seat, wishing this would all just end. Her story was driving itself into me like a thousand needles, filling my head with a million different possibilities.

Eventually, she was able to continue. "I watched him die, putting him through that awful death. I killed him and freed myself. A few moments later and I was rushing for the surface, my body returned to me and my life restored. I left him in that crushing darkness and I..."

A short pause, then a scream, like a wounded animal dying in agony.

"I LAUGHED! I laughed like I'd never laughed a day in my life. I laughed because I was alive and I laughed because I had just killed the only person who I loved in this world. And after that... I never laughed again."

She wiped her eyes and looked at me with an air of finality.

"That lake is cursed. You think it kills people, but it doesn't. It traps them. And the only way you can escape is if you trap someone else."

She got up and quietly opened the front door. I followed her in a daze. My eyes went back to that picture on the shelf and I remembered why it looked familiar...

The stranger that came out of the water.

I reached the door and she looked at me one last time, those years of sadness and guilt etched into her skin. "Now get the fuck out of my house."

Esther killed herself yesterday. No one would have known if her neighbors hadn't heard the gunshot, I'm sure. They found a man inside trying in vain to put back the broken pieces of her head, sobbing and calling her name. They took him in for questioning. I wonder what they'll think when they find his name is Alan Manchester. I wonder why it took him so long to find her... but none of that matters, now. It's too late for them, anyway.

As for me, I have made my decision.

I wrote Liz a letter. Her parents let me go into her room when I told them it would make me feel better to see it one last time. I'm kind of like a second daughter to them, anyway, so they didn't even hesitate. I left the letter under her pillow where she likes to hide her books when she pretends to sleep. I hope she'll find it soon after she gets home.

I would do anything for Liz. We may be best friends, but we're closer than sisters or lovers. We're as close as two people can possibly be. I think back now to what Esther said it was like, tossing and turning in those dark waters, searching for your body and never finding it.

Liz didn't have a choice, but I do.

I love you, Liz. Please remember to tell my parents that I love them, too.

It's time to go swimming.

CHAPTER 8.

ALL IN A DAY'S WORK

"The usual?"

"The usual."

I sat at the bar, waiting on my beer and watching the college football game play out on the big, flatscreen TV. The bar was pretty much empty. Well, it was a Wednesday afternoon, after all, so you couldn't really expect too many people. Most people would be headed home to rest before the next day's work, unable to afford any of the heavy drinking that the majority of them came here to do. But me, I liked the clear atmosphere of a quiet bar. It was a good place to decompress after a hard day's work at the construction site, and that happened to be what I needed on that particular afternoon.

Lou was just handing me my beer when the door opened and a young man slunk up to the bar and took the seat next to mine. His voice was quiet, so quiet I almost couldn't hear it, as he ordered a whiskey on the rocks and stared off into space. A few husky fellas started a game of pool, crowding around the table with hearty laughter. Alabama scored a touchdown on the tube in a rerun of last week's game.

I gotta admit, I was a little miffed to have company. It had been a long, hard day, what with a newbie on the job who could barely hold a hammer properly much less operate any of the heavy machinery. All I really wanted to do was nurse my beer for half an hour before I had to head home to my wife. Not that she's so bad, really, it's just that our apartment is pretty damn small and it's nice to have a little time to myself. A few moments to clear my head and quiet my own grumbing, otherwise I'd head home complaining. My wife, she hates that. Too much negativity, she'd say. So I had to get it out here, in the peace and quiet of my own thoughts. And when a guy sits right next to you at an empty bar like this, it means he wants to talk and, quite frankly, I wasn't feeling like it that day.

But as I sipped my beer and watched Alabama run the ball again, I took closer notice of the guy. He looked rough, real rough, like he'd just caught his wife in bed with the milkman. His face was haggard and pale. He kept running his hands through his brown hair, brown and a little long for my tastes. He stared down hard at the glossy wood counter. Most importantly, he was knocking his whiskey back as though it could save his life. One, two, three shots, all down the hatch. Bottoms up.

Now, truth be told, I've always been a bit of a lightweight. All the other guys in construction used to give me shit for it when we went out for drinks after work. It really sorta bugged me, you know? Tough as nails but a little bitch when it comes to holding my booze. So, you see, I couldn't help but notice this guy chugging away his liquor without a second thought.

Despite my earlier reservations, I felt like I had to talk to this guy. I mean, he looked like he really needed it, like something was really eating away at him. And I like to think of myself as a personable fellow. Warm and engaging, that's what my wife calls me. I felt that I had a responsibility to my fellow man or something. That was my trouble. So I opened my mouth. I opened my damn mouth.

"Rough day at work?"

"Yeah." He was still staring down at the table, his hands playing nervously with his glass. Man, I hate that. Fidgeting, that is.

I shoulda just stopped right then and there, but he looked like he was gonna snap at any minute. I really felt sorry for the guy, couldn't just leave him to sit and stew like that. "Well, everyone has days like that."

"Not like this."

I waited quietly for an explanation, but it became pretty clear that he wasn't gonna give one to me. Well, screw him. I had a family to get home to. A little family, but it was mine all the same. I was about to give up for good and go home when he decided I was worth talking to again.

"There will be more."

His tone was real strange, much calmer than the rest of him, which was shaking like a leaf. Suddenly, I wanted very much to finish my drink and head home. I bet if I asked, my wife, Sarah, would cook me my favorite food, spaghetti with thick sauce, homemade, not the shit you buy in a jar at the store. She's good to me like that, always treating me to the little things. Things that I should appreciate more, I know. So, I tried to lead him around to the end of the conversation so I could leave without feeling too guilty. "Well, why don't you just quit, then?"

"Not many people can do what I do."

I felt a little stab of annoyance. I sized him up. He was wearing a black suit and tie, crisp undershirt and shined up shoes. Real expensive. Probably some fancy salaryman, calculating figures for a Fortune 500 company, too good for the likes of a manual laborer like me. Now I really wanted to get the hell out of there.

"Well, if it's such an important job, then you must be an important man for doing it. Let me guess, something that takes a lot of schooling, a lot of preparation, not something your everyday chump like me can do, hm? Well, I don't think you'd have gone through all that work to get where you are just to fail. A bad day is a bad day. Accept it and get on with your life."

I don't like to brag, of course, but I like to think that I know what to say. When someone's upset, when someone's looking for advice, I know what to say. This guy, he just needed someone to stroke his ego. Usually so confident, so sure of himself, but still sort of delicate. Not the sort of guy I try to spend a lot of time with. A stumbling block in his oh-so-carefully chosen career that's made him question everything about himself for perhaps the first time. Preen over him for a while and he'll be back to normal.

While I was thinking this, Mr. Important Salaryman started to nod to himself, his eyes growing wide. He stopped fidgeting with his glass – thank God – and his lips parted as he breathed heavily. He looked deep in thought, lost on the train tracks of his own mind. I caught Lou's eye in the hopes of paying the tab and getting the hell out of there.

"Three bucks."

"For a beer? You're fuckin' kidding me, you bloodsucker."

It was our usual banter but I could hear the edge in my own voice today. I handed over a fiver and stood up to go. As I turned away from the bar, Alabama fumbled the ball and the man grabbed me by my arm.

"Hey, for what it's worth, thanks a lot. That really helped."

He looked at me with such honest gratitude that I couldn't help but feel my attitude soften towards him just a bit. Probably not such a bad guy after all, just a little different than me. And that was ok. The world needs people like him, too, after all.

I was about to go when I stopped and thought for a half a minute. I stared at that long brown hair, toying with something on the tip of my tongue. If I could've anticipated his answer, I never would have asked the question.

"Say, just out of curiosity... what is it that you do, anyway?"

He looked over at me with a sort of rueful smile that had just a touch of pride. He downed his last whiskey and I watched it drained measuredly into his mouth. The huskier of the fellas won the pool game. Alabama had the ball back.

"I'm a mortician. Today I embalmed my first child."

CHAPTER 9.

SISSY'S EYES

Light, fluffy blue, floating like lilies in the whites of her eyes. Those are what my sister's eyes look like. I was always envious of them when I was a kid. I had these dull, grey eyes that no one took any notice of. But Sissy's eyes... they were really something. Lovely and enchanting, like something out of a Disney movie.

Sissy is what I call my sister. No, that's not her actual name, and yes, I really do call her that. And for the sake of anonymity, that's how it will remain for this story.

And this story is about Sissy's eyes.

Sissy is seven years older than I am. We're closer than most sisters, probably because she's moved out and graduated from college so I don't have to share a room with her anymore, the neat freak. She lives a state away in The Big City. We come from a small town of about two thousand people, so any town is big to us, if I'm being completely honest. She lives in a city of about 300,000 people and I love to visit her. She takes me out to see plays, eat at fancy restaurants, hang out with her friends, and even go ghost hunting (she knows I'm a nut for the supernatural). Plus, now that I'm seventeen, she buys us booze and lets me drink (so long as I have a glass of water between every drink, she doesn't want me to be sick). Having a big sister is awesome.

It's the last time that I visited her where things got a little strange.

Mom dropped me off with my duffel bag at Sissy's door. Mom and Dad were visiting my older brother, and Sissy's apartment is on the way. She rushed me inside and helped me get situated in her room – even now that we're so much older we still share a bed when I stay over.

She made us spaghetti (the only thing she can make without burning, really) and we talked excitedly about what we'd do for the week that I was staying with her. Of course we'd go see that new horror movie that had allegedly already given a few viewers heart attacks, and then we'd go to the mall, and what night should we stay in and order pizza...

After our meal, I pulled up my Netflix and searched for Bridezillas (our guilty pleasure). She stood up and headed for the bathroom.

"Where are you going?" I called out.

"I'm going to take out my eyes!" she teased. I scowled.

It's a pretty famous story in my family. It happened when Sissy was thirteen and I was six.

Sissy has beautiful eyes but they don't work as well as they could. As a result, she's had contacts for as long as I can remember. She refuses to wear glasses, probably because she's the fashionista out of the two of us and wouldn't be caught dead with rims obstructing her pretty face.

Anyway, one night I walked into the bathroom while Sissy was taking out her contacts. Only I didn't realize that was what she was doing. To me, it looked like she was preparing to pluck out those pretty little eyeballs. I started screaming, startling Sissy from her nightly routine and causing mom to rush into the bathroom.

"What happened, sweetie?"

"Jesus, Maddie, what's with you?"

Mom ignored my sister's overly-liberal use of the J-word as she tried to calm me down. After a few moments of hitching breath and false starts, I managed to choke out, "Sissy was taking her eyes out!"

My mom, bless her soul, tried to keep a straight face but broke down as soon as my sister broke out in hysterics. Mom laughed and hugged me and gave me some ice cream, soothing me while explaining what had Sissy was actually doing.

At least, this is the story as it has been related to me over the years. I was only six and I don't happen to remember any of it, so it must not have been all that scarring. To be honest, I think the story has probably gotten exaggerated over years of retelling.

But after Sissy's allusion to my supposed childhood trauma, I found myself more aware of my own eyes than usual. In fact, they seemed a little dry. I walked to the bathroom and knocked on the door.

Sissy opened up. I didn't see any of the contact supplies on the sink.

"I thought you were 'taking out your eyes'?"

She looked back absentmindedly, "Oh, yeah, I think I'll have to wait until later, actually."

Well, whatever. "Hey, can I borrow some contact solution? Or some eye drops? My eyes are kind of dry."

She looked at me a little funny. "No contact solution, but I might have eye drops."

What the hell? How did she not have contact solution? Then I realized that must be why she wasn't taking her contacts out yet. She must have run out. Typical of her not to buy it until the very last second. She handed me some eye drops and they did the trick. After a little more sisterly banter we marathoned Bridezillas and passed out around one in the morning.

I had a terrible nightmare.

In my nightmare, I saw our old cat, Spook. He was a black cat that we'd had for a few years as a kid, only to die upon eating something poisoned from the fields after they'd just been sprayed. Spook was staring up at me, his black fur sleek and smooth just like I remember it.

"Hey, Spook." I reached out to pet him, when suddenly, his face shifted.

He reached up a sharp claw and swatted at his face. What the hell was he doing? I'd never seen him do that before. My hand faltered as I watched nervously.

He swiped and swiped until his claws caught onto his eyes. His claws hooked through the yellow slits, drawing blood and white ooze as he yanked his paw back. He repeated this motion until all that was left in his skull were red gouges, streaming with puss and blood. He mewled serenely, licking the blood from his claws, his tail twitching.

I screamed.

I woke up in a state of panic. My eyes adjusted to the dark, although everything remained sort of out of focus. I felt a dull pain growing ever sharper behind my eyes. What the fuck? I rubbed them, but it seemed to make the pain worse, if anything. I looked over to the side of the bed. Sissy wasn't there. She was probably in the bathroom.

I headed over to the bathroom in order to get the eye drops again. Man, my eyes were killing me. The light was on and the door was ajar. Sissy was humming quietly to herself, she must have had her iPod in. I padded down the hallway in bare feet, desperate for some relief.

I pulled the bathroom door open. And that's when I saw it.

Sissy was leaning over the sink, the drain wide open and the water already running. She was holding her eyelids open, waiting. She looked ridiculous and a touch stupid. I was about to snarkily ask her what the hell she was doing when I noticed...

Her left eye... it twitched. It trembled in the socket. It was almost imperceptible at first and I thought I was imagining it, and then...

It wiggled.

It slithered. It crawled.

"Come on," Sissy muttered. She used her purple manicured pointer finger to prod at the eyeball, causing it to shudder violently.

And then it dropped.

It plopped into the sink, followed by a string of veins, blood, and white puss. She blinked her eye a few times as the oozing mess dripped down the drain, sliding along the white porcelain of the sink like cottage cheese. I saw bright red where her eye should be, and then watched in horror as the right eye followed suit.

Plop. White and red sludge, with a tinge of the blue that I had always admired.

Sissy closed her eyelids for a few moments, still leaning over the sink. When she opened them, I saw new eyes, blue and perfectly identical to the ones before them, pushing into place. They slithered and slipped into their proper holes. She blinked a few times, as though to adjust them.

She pulled out her earphones and heard my ragged breathing. She turned around in surprise.

"Hey, Maddie, what's up? Do you need some more eye drops?"

I felt sick. I thought I might throw up. I wanted to scream but I fought down the urge as much as I could. I opened my mouth and my voice trembled out.

"What the fuck, Sissy? What the fuck, I don't... what the FUCK?!"

I started to cry and hyperventilate. To my surprise, she rolled her freshly-grown eyes at me. "Payback for the joke I made earlier? Geez, I know that you're a late bloomer, but you'll get your first soon, too, so stop obsessing over it, ok?"

I only had a moment to wonder what the fuck she was talking about before I felt my left eye twitch.

CHAPTER 10.

THE ICE KING AND HIS PRINCESS

Growing up on a small acreage in Minnesota certainly had its perks: there was a vast grove behind the house to mess around in, tractors to climb and explore, barns to build forts in, grain bins to scale when our mom wasn't looking... there was no end to the trouble that we three kids could find if we really set our minds to it.

Of course, there were a few downfalls.

For example, it could, at times, feel pretty isolated. We were three miles outside of the nearest town, and even that town only had about a thousand people to its name. Sometimes it felt like living at the edge of the world, where the wind was never just a breeze but always carried a bitter chill of indifference.

This isolation was made all the worse by my dad's job. Being a state trooper, I'd always looked up to him as a kid. I liked to admire his squad car and would often sit outside the house as he drove off to work, waiting for those few occasions where he would flash those red and blue lights for me. Playing with his state issued hat and messing with the intercom in the squad was all great fun... until, that is, he had to go to work, and I'd be left wondering if he was ever coming back.

Due to the nature of my father's job, my family was sometimes the target of threats, usually from the local alcoholics he'd dumped in jail overnight for drunk driving. And, as far as I can recall, none of the threats ever really amounted to anything. For the most part, the worst it got were a few phone calls, leading to a period of time where us kids weren't allowed to answer the phone. Every few months we'd have to buy a new mailbox, too, but that wasn't really so bad. It just meant that we had to be extra careful.

Usually, we were very, very careful. But sometimes, things just slip through the cracks.

When I was about seven we had a particularly harsh winter. The temperature dropped into the -50°F range, leading to a statewide shut down. Soon the winds came, carrying heavy snow with them. Minnesota became white and glittering and deadly. As the snow piled up, my father went out to work, sentenced to about three days of pulling idiots from the ditch non-stop.

We knew when he barely managed to pull out of our snow-cushioned driveway that he wouldn't be home until the blizzard was over. As such, we were all a bit depressed. I was particularly worried because from a young age my father had pounded into my brain just how dangerous these winter roads can be. In the back of my mind, I kept on wondering what he might see out on the roads that night.

Mom set out sleeping bags downstairs, as the upstairs of our house was neither heated nor properly insulated, and popped in a Disney movie as she threw in a pizza for supper. That, at least, was something to look forward to. I was also looking forward to snuggling between my older brother and sister when a loud pounding came at the door.

My mom almost never let unexpected visitors into the house. If a car showed up in the middle of the night unannounced, she would grab the shotgun immediately and sit at the foot of the stairs, guarding us kids with her life. Many nights in the earlier years of my parents' marriage she'd sit like that until dad came home, even if the car left without notice or trouble.

But in the winter, all the rules changed.

Sometimes, when people get stranded on those snowy Minnesota roads, they end up leaving their cars to search for help. That is always a terrible decision. Each year a few people end up frozen to death, an icy grave in a barren ditch the last memory they ever leave behind. Few people who abandon one shelter ever make it to another.

So you must understand, when someone knocks on your door in the middle of a blizzard, you answer. Their life could depend on it.

But I know my mom hesitated. Us kids crept into the kitchen to watch as mom stood before the door, her hand hovering above the doorknob.

I wanted to call out to her, ask her what she was going to do, but my sister silenced me with a pert finger pressed against her lips. We waited in silence as mom turned the lock with deft fingers and pulled open the door.

Although my mother's small frame was blocking our view, I could see his towering frame filling the doorway. He was tall and sturdy, dressed in a heavy winter jacket, a fur hat pulled down around his ears. Long, black hair hung around his face, dusted with a quiet frost. As my mother stepped aside and let him into the house, I managed to catch a glimpse of his eyes through that curtain of hair. They were deep and dark, and I instantly mentally assigned him the name Ice King.

He removed his heavy thunking boots and thick farmer's gloves, following my mom to the living room and sitting himself down next to the fireplace. I couldn't help thinking how strange it looked, the imposing Ice King seated in front of our tiny little fireplace, rubbing his hands and watching me.

He hadn't noticed my brother or sister, but he was staring right at me. And I was staring back.

I could tell he was making my mom nervous, as she tried to usher us kids out of the room. But then, all of a sudden, his grim stone face broke into a smile and those tar black eyes danced into life like the tip of a flame.

"Oh, don't mind me, I love kids! I have a few little ones of my own at home. In fact, one is a little girl, just about your age!" He jabbed a rough, dirt-encrusted finger in my direction and gave me a goofy smile. Something about him was just infectious, and soon I was in a fit of giggles.

Gradually, mom relaxed as the guy chattered on with us kids. He was very charismatic, his smile seeming to invade everything around him. Pretty soon, even my mom was joking and laughing along with him. He sat with us kids and told us stories about his adventures all over the world. Now that I think back on it, he definitely made it all up, but his stories were so amazing that I couldn't get enough. One minute he was a grizzled old pirate, sailing the seven seas with a death wish and a lust for gold. The next, he was a gentlemen studying in England, courting a stuffy English woman whose father didn't approve of his gruff voice and coarse skin. Whatever tale he spun fell like gold around my ears.

Although he played with my brother and sister as well, he seemed most interested in me. He pulled me onto his lap as the Little Mermaid played in the background, tickling me and playing with my hair. I loved the attention. I loved being special. He kept calling me "Little Princess"... I was the princess of the Ice King.

After a while us kids got tired and mom put us into our sleeping bags. She had a hell of a time separating me from Ice King. Although my mom held her arms out to me, my arms clung around his thick neck and refused to let go. She had to wait until I was tired enough to loosen my grip before she could free him.

Ice King slept on the couch and my mom opted to stay on the floor next to us kids. Thinking back, I'm sure she intended to stay up all night with us, just in case. No matter how sweet the man seemed, it was still better to remain cautious.

Only she didn't stay awake. She must have passed out after a few hours of struggling against the weight of her eyes.

When I woke up it was around three in the morning. The wind howled around the house and it was pitch black outside, no moonlight to illuminate the ghostly snow. I looked around sleepily and noticed a light glowing from the kitchen.

I toddled towards the kitchen, hoping for a glass of water when I saw Ice King sitting on the floor.

That first stone cold expression was engrained into his eyes again, but this time I noticed his face was wet with tears, the outer edges of his eyes singed red. He was sitting with his back against the door, staring into his hands. My eyes followed his gaze naturally and fell upon a small pistol that he was turning over and over...

I was frozen in place. This was definitely wrong.

Ice King raised his head and looked at me, the black jewels of his eyes resting against the light blue of my own. The gun danced in the palm of his hand, pointed carelessly towards me. I shuddered.

"Should I take you with me? Would that be better?"

I couldn't answer. My own fear had settled into my throat and turned me mute, even though the rest of my body wanted to scream for my mom. Instead, I simply watched as he lifted the gun towards his mouth.

He smiled at me one last time, but that sparkling flame had already been snuffed out. "Bye, bye, Little Princess."

His blood was all over the door and my mom was at my side in a minute. I think she managed to keep my siblings from seeing the gore but it was too late for me. I spent some hours in a therapist's office after that, trying to get over what I'd seen. For months I had nightmares about the gaping hole where the back of his head should have been.

My dad ended up being one of the officers that worked the case. Usually, cops don't work cases when their own family is involved, but this time they made an exception. Because of this, he knew everything about what happened. It wasn't until tonight, fourteen years later and two years after his retirement, that a glass of scotch had loosened his lips enough to tell me.

Ice King – that had been my name for him. In actuality, he was a man named Frederick Mansfield, 37 at the time of his death, with a wife and two children... already deceased.

A few winters before, his wife had made a bad decision. Their car had gone off the road during a blizzard and although they'd waited for a few hours, help had yet to come. She bundled up the two-year-old and took the seven-year-old by her tiny, gloved hand out into the Minnesota snow.

They were found less than half a mile from their car and they were less than a quarter of a mile from the nearest house.

They almost made it.

His wife had tried to shield her children the best she could, but despite her efforts they had all succumbed to the cold eventually, frozen in position and painted with frost like little porcelain dolls.

After the death of his wife and children, the Ice King moved further south towards our neck of the woods. The pain of his loss must have followed him, though, because only a few years later he took his own car out in one of Minnesota's worst blizzards in recent memory and drove it straight into the ditch, as if he had meant to do it. My father's guess is that he never intended to make it home that night.

He left his car for the freezing night, hoping to join his children and his wife, either through the cold or the gritty metal of his pistol. Instead, he happened to stumble upon our house and was unable to resist the urge to sample its warmth just once for himself.

In the end, I think we did him one last favor. I can still remember those twinkling eyes as they stared at me, as though they were trying to imprint something into his memory. Now I think it wasn't me he was looking at. I think, for that one night, we became his family, taking their place in those last few hours before he went to meet them.

I'll never have any proof of my theory, other than this: after my father told me this story, I looked online for more information on his wife and children. Along with the obituaries and news stories, I found a picture of his seven-year-old daughter's tombstone. I saw my proof etched on the front.

In Memory of My Little Princess.

CHAPTER 11.

MY ENCOUNTERS WITH THOSE PEOPLE

When I was a child, my mother used to talk a lot about Those People.

When dad drove us to get ice cream after Sunday morning mass, mom would spy a group of teenage guys messing around on their skateboards and start muttering about the "godlessness of Those People." Sometimes she'd spit it at a single mother who had the gall to be coddling her baby in public. I admit that as a child, I didn't really know who Those People were supposed to be: my mother seemed to consign everyone different from us to that dangerous group.

Of course, there are some differences that children are unable to see.

When I was about seven or eight, I was waiting outside the elementary school for my mom to come pick me up from school. She was late again and most of the other students had already gone home. I was sitting on the sidewalk, playing with a hapless ladybug that had crossed my path, when a tall man in a long, dark coat approached me.

I don't remember him very well, but I remember long, shaggy hair and dirty hands. I was wary of him at first – mom had always been firm about teaching me not to talk to strangers. But he told me he was there to pick up his daughter and I relaxed a little. We started chatting and he told me all about his dog who had just had puppies. He'd gladly sell me one if I only went home with him to pick it up, he said.

He had taken me by the hand when my mom pulled up in our big minivan and started screaming and shouting at him. After that, all I remember is being scared, clinging to my mom as she and the man snarled at each other. He was still snarling as she threw me into the car and swerved off.

I was positive I was going to get in trouble, but when we pulled into our driveway she just pulled me into her arms and held me for a while. She made me promise not to talk to any strange men again. Then she brought me in the house and that was the end of that.

That was my first encounter with Those People.

―――――――――――

My second encounter came just as I was entering high school. I was a gangly freshman with braces and woefully stringy hair that seemed to stay greasy no matter now often I washed it. My family had moved for about the millionth time – my father's job takes him all around the US – so I had no friends or even acquaintances in this new town. As a result, I joined as many teams and clubs as I could, determined not to be the one high schooler who didn't have any friends.

Most of the clubs I ended up dropping out of – turns out I didn't have any aptitude for public speaking, acting, cheerleading, or painting. Much to my surprise, however, I had a real knack for running. I stayed on our school track team and, over the course of the next few weeks, broke several school records.

I really enjoyed the track meets, hanging out with my new friends and sailing around the track at light speed. But then around the fourth or fifth meet, I started to notice a regular spectator who only seemed to watch me.

He was just vaguely familiar at first. It took me a while to correctly place that shaggy hair and coarse skin. He didn't have the long, black coat anymore, but he had a wide-brimmed hat hiding his face. He would stand at the edge of the football field fence, always watching me.

At first, I didn't mention anything to my parents. After all, he wasn't bothering me. Furthermore, it couldn't be the same man: we'd moved at least ten times since that near-forgotten childhood nightmare.

I kept it quiet until one day when it wasn't just him. Accompanying him at the fence was a petite but chesty woman with long dark hair, along with another man who had blaringly white skin. They were all dressed in black.

And they were all watching me.

I told my mom that night and she seemed to brush the incident off. Don't worry about it, she told me. It's just your imagination. But the pallor that came into her cheeks betrayed her worry. I didn't go to school that next week, and we moved to another state the next weekend.

End of story.

The story picked back up a few weeks ago. I'm a freshman at college now, a nice little private school that just about cost me my soul to get into. Things were going well and I was having a pretty normal college experience, the perfect cocktail of studying, stress, boys, and parties.

One night my roommates dragged me to an off-campus house party. It promised lots of booze and lots of creepy guys, but the booze was free and my roommates could always be counted on for good company.

It was around one in the morning when I saw him sitting across the room. I had drunk myself pretty well into a stupor by this point and I was floating high, walking among the black clouds of the night sky. When I spotted him this time, my mind was lucid enough to make the connection almost immediately. My roommates, similarly drunk off their asses, didn't notice me swaying to my feet and sauntering across the room to where he was seated in an overstuffed old armchair.

"You... why d'you follow me?" I slurred, just your typical, drunk, white college girl. "Don't pretend y'don' know what I'm talking 'bout!" I admonished. "I r'member you..." At that point, my memory cuts off, which is a pretty good indication that I'd passed out.

I must have been out for a few hours, because when I came to I felt entirely sober. I was in a dark, smoky room, lying on what felt like concrete. I blinked a few times and as I adjusted to darkness, I saw an array of rusty machines looming over me. I tried to sit up but found I couldn't move. Shock hit me first when I tried to move my hands and found them bound behind my back. A similar feeling of restraint was found accompanying my ankles and knees. I wiggled around a little bit but was pretty well trussed up. The panic didn't hit until I tried to scream and found I'd been gagged.

A flame sparked off in the darkness. I strained my eyes, feeling like a rabbit caught in a trap. The little flame settled on what appeared to be a candle. Instead of relief, that small light cultivated a thread of dread inside of me.

One by one, a circle of candles were lit around me. I shuddered as the room lit up and I could see something red painted on the floor around me. I didn't know what that meant, but I imagined it couldn't be anything good. The ropes were starting to cut off my circulation and I could feel bruises forming around my wrists where I had been pulling wildly. My first coherent thought since waking up formed in my brain: this was bad. Really, really bad.

My heart beat wildly as a loud, booming voice started to bounce off the machinery and fill the cavernous space I'd found myself in. I couldn't figure out what it was saying, or what language it was in. It sounded strangely nonsensical, yet rhythmic and almost alive. All I knew for sure was that it emanated from the man in black, the one who had pursued me after all this time.

I cycled between terror and unease as I tried to make sense of what was happening. An arrangement of black-cloaked statue-like attendants stood in a careful circle, with one cloak behind each candle. I wished desperately that someone would just for one second speak English, for the love of God say SOMETHING I understand, then I'll have found my footing, then I can...

My brain stopped babbling the moment I saw my stalker lift a knife out of his own cloak. It was long and I imagined it was razor sharp. The handle was blood red and encrusted with beautiful stones. I squirmed even harder as he stepped towards me, but there was nowhere to go, not even if I could move. He knelt down next to me and placed a rough hand on my cheek. He looked into my eyes and I looked right back.

I wish I could say I saw something human in those eyes, or something inhuman, or something strange, or something... at all. But looking into those eyes was like looking at a blank slate. It was like looking at someone that didn't exist at all, not in the way that mattered.

He brought the thin blade up to my neck and continued chanting. My heart was beating so fast that it felt like one continuous scream in my chest. Tears bathed my cheeks and I wondered which feeling was going to be my last: my heart, the knife, or my tears.

Suddenly, shots rang through the air and I blacked out.

I woke up in the hospital, a tiny slice on my throat but otherwise unharmed. I felt blurry and muddled at first. I was hooked up to an IV so I could safely assume they'd given me a sedative of some sort. My mom was crying. I wondered vaguely if Those People had made her cry.

It wasn't until my consciousness fully returned that my mother, her cheeks burning with shame, her hand clenched firmly in my father's, managed to tell me an old story that she'd buried away in her chest.

When my mother was about my age, she'd gotten mixed up with Those People. See, she'd fallen in love with a man, Darius Hick, and he had coaxed her into a world of alcohol, drugs, sex, and the occult. It had started off innocent enough: Ouija boards, tarot cards, séances, the like.

But then Darius used his honey lips and sweet words to introduce my mother to a Satanic cult. At least, they called themselves Satanic: whatever they were was far darker than anything she'd encountered then or since. At first, she was so drugged out of her mind that she wasn't alarmed. Besides, for a while, it was mostly talk. They'd talk about blood and sacrifices and demons and spells. And she'd sit in Darius's lap and look into those deep brown eyes.

But things changed when she found out she was pregnant. She'd been excited at first, and Darius was, too. But she soon found herself ill at ease when he made her promise to give him her first-born as an offering of love.

Now, it happened that one of the other women in the cult had recently given birth as well. And one night in the early stages of her pregnancy, Darius and the cult held a special ceremony.

My mother choked up at this point – she wouldn't tell me exactly what happened. But from what I gathered, the child was given up as a sacrifice. A sacrifice to something dark and unspeakable, to something (imagined?) that the cult worshipped.

She ran away that night.

She tried to report the cult to the police, too terrified to hide her own involvement in their activities up until the sacrifice. As soon as the police arrived at their hideout, however, they found the place ransacked and abandoned. My mother was immediately placed in witness protection. The investigation continued indefinitely, but the cult had never been apprehended.

A few years later, my mother met Stephen Winchester. They fell in love and married. He shouldered her troubled past and offered her a place in him to purify her heart.

They were happy until Darius came looking for that first-born to complete his sacrifice.

My mother couldn't continue after that, but it didn't matter: the rest of the story was already written in my memory.

In the end, I was incredibly lucky. A sober boy at the party saw me being carried out by Darius and called the police. The police had been watching some of Darius's accomplices for months, noting certain specific violent incidents that they no doubt had a hand in. As soon as they got the call, they stormed the hideout – and old abandoned factory just off the main highway – and found me playing the part of the unwilling sacrificial lamb.

They tell me that Darius was shot in the raid. They tell me all the other cult members were either shot along with him or are in custody. They tell me that I don't have to be afraid anymore.

But I still lock my door whenever I get back to my dorm. I still look carefully around every corner, wondering who might be hiding in the shadows.

And I still have nightmares every night.

The nightmare is always the same: in it, I am surrounded by an unspeakable, impenetrable darkness. I feel my screaming heart, my own hot tears, but nothing else.

And then I hear Darius say the first sentence he ever directed at me: "I'm here to pick up my daughter from school."

CHAPTER 12.

DON'T BRING US BACK

I do not have any wise words to say about death.

I think that, before I experienced it, I would have been able to write so many pretty words, so many desperate phrases justifying its cruelty. Something to comfort the mothers who have lost their daughters, the children who have watched their parents fade away. In the past, I was naïve enough to think that I could spin words like these.

So what CAN I tell you about death? That it is only as extraordinary and strange as life. Dying did not hurt, not for me. The cancer? That hurt. But slipping away into another existence was as natural as swimming. And slowly coming into a new consciousness, that wasn't painful, either. It wasn't scary or strange. It was all very natural.

Death itself was kind of blissful, actually. Does that make you feel better? I imagine it doesn't. Because the real pain is felt by those who are left behind. It is strange that there is no pain or grief in death. Grief doesn't make sense in the afterlife. The afterlife is mostly just waiting. What pain is there in waiting when the outcome is certain?

So there you have it. Death isn't that bad. At least not if I'm to be believed. But how do you know that you can trust me? After all, dead girls don't write stories.

But I'm not dead anymore.

You see, when I got cancer, I was only 28. I lasted until 32. I was unlucky, you know. They say that pretty soon people won't die of cancer anymore, but pretty soon didn't come fast enough for me. In the papers, they probably said something like:

"Anastasia Richards passed away last Sunday, leaving behind a husband, Thomas Richards, 36, and two daughters, Amanda, 8, and Grace, 4."

I wish obituaries wouldn't use terms like "leaving behind." It doesn't seem quite fair to say that we've left people behind. It's not like we wanted to do it, at least not in most cases.

I'm sorry. Everything is kind of jumbled up in my head and I'm in so much pain. It's hard to put this down into words that actually make sense.

Anyway, when I got sick, I knew how hard this would be on my family. I knew that they would suffer. And I really, really wished they didn't have to. But there was nothing I could do. I was going to hurt them, and that was how the story ended.

But there was something I didn't expect. See, I hoped that Thomas, my Thomas, would stay strong. I liked to imagine that he would find the strength to carry on. He'd get married again, probably, and the girls would have another mother, someone to take care of them while I was gone. Those thoughts didn't make me happy but they did give me peace.

I didn't expect that Thomas would break down. Now, mind you, the dead can't see the living. But when I started feeling that awful pain, I knew something was wrong.

It is hard to describe that pain because I didn't have a body anymore. But imagine this: you're sleeping, very peacefully, when you start to feel a fire spreading out through your veins. It spreads down to your stomach and up to your head. The heat becomes even more intense and it feels like you're cooking alive. And just when you think you can't bear it anymore, everything splits open, like a thousand knives are raking through your skin.

And you can't even scream.

I couldn't scream for so long and the pain just never ended. And then all of a sudden there was air. And there were lungs and hands clutching at a chest, and I could feel them all, and they were MINE. I was screaming and it was my own voice.

And there was an awful sinking feeling that I was *alive*.

I opened my eyes and saw the ruins of my own house. Everything was dark and filthy. There was an awful smell saturating the air, like the trash hadn't been taken out in weeks. Dust motes swirled through the dank air as I coughed myself back to life.

Sitting to the right was my husband. The way he was, I almost didn't recognize him. He hadn't shaved since I'd died, that much was clear, although you couldn't say he'd managed to grow a beard. There was just a wild tangle of hair covering his face. His eyes were far off and milky, like something had been spilled in them. He was holding a ragged book in his hand with a leathery surface. I didn't want to know what that was or why he appeared to be reading from it. My eyes drifted to the corner of the room, where my two daughters cowered.

They looked like they hadn't eaten in months. My oldest was covered in bumps and scrapes. Her eyes were wild like her father's, but still more present, more aware. My youngest was on the verge of fainting, her body limp against her sister's.

And through all this, the pain still writhed. As I looked down at my own body, I was horrified to see the rot settled in my own skin. It looked as though the rot was slowly healing, falling away. But in exchange I was enduring the most dreadful pain I'd ever felt.

The pain was maddening – I would have done anything to end it. No, dying didn't hurt... but being dragged back into life was torture.

I sat up. Every movement was dreadful, but I was fueled by confusion and fear and this burning anger, this rage.

"Thomas." My voice was gravelly and shaky, but it was my own. Thomas stopped his reading and stared at me with wide, trembling eyes.

"It worked... oh, oh, it worked, you... you're alive!"

Maybe you'll think I should have felt love for him. After all, he was my husband 'til death did us part. But at that moment, he didn't seem like my husband at all. My husband wasn't there any more... and I felt nothing for this beast. I felt only that boiling anger at the pain I was experiencing.

"Thomas. What did you do?" I continued to pull air into my lungs, but I wished I would stop. I wished everything would just stop.

"I brought you back, sweetie. I brought you home. Now we can be happy again, right girls?" Thomas's voice carried the tone of a threat and I saw my oldest wince.

I can't really explain what happened next. Thomas tried to put his arms around me. The smell of my own rot reached into my nostrils. I heard my youngest daughter start coughing. I heard my oldest trying to shush her.

I felt my rage boil over.

I don't know where I got my strength, but I jumped against Thomas, pushing him down to the ground. He was surprised but not resisting: he wasn't Thomas anymore, he was something else entirely. So I didn't feel particularly plagued with guilt when I felt my hands grasp the sides of his head and wrench hard to the left. I was shocked at the strength in my limbs: I'd been so weak when I died. But my husband's neck had all the resistance of a straw. He was alive one moment and dead the next.

Killing him helped a little, but that burning, searing pain still ripped through my body, and now my rage had no outlet. Not until I saw Amanda strike Grace for whimpering a little too loudly.

I lunged. Amanda screamed but she was too weak to really do anything. My anger was burning bright and hot. She'd already been ruined by her father. What had he done to them? I bashed her frail body against the wall. It only took one good hit to kill her. She struggled a little, but in the end, she went easily.

The pain was still terrible, but my anger was starting to abate. I had one moment of horrible realization, one second of insane guilt, before the rational side of my mind took over. I'd done what any sane person would do in this situation, hadn't I? They were suffering and nothing could repair the damage that my death had done. Just because my death was reversed doesn't mean their pain could be. I'd delivered them to a place of peace, a place with no suffering.

My little Grace was still shaking in the corner, but I could see that she was on the verge of death even without my murderous rage. I picked up her tiny body, struggling against the fire in my veins, and stared at her wide, blurred eyes.

"Mommy?"

I tried to block out that lilting question as I snapped her neck like her father's. I felt like crying but I held my tears back: I'd be joining them soon enough.

I'm planning on dying now, too. I scoured the house and found my husband's pistol. He'd left my computer alone, too. In fact, he'd left everything of mine as it was when I passed. As soon as it had enough charge, I opened up to a word processing document, where you're reading this now, no doubt.

You all need to know. This is not a joke, this is not a game. Life is not a game. Everyone in this world has lost somebody... somebody they desperately want back. But as this pain whips through my body and I eye that pistol like candy, I can tell you at least this: if you bring us back, you bring us back to pain and suffering. The dead are better off where they are.

Don't bring us back.

CHAPTER 13.

AN UNCONVENTIONAL ADOPTION

When my husband, Dave, and I moved into our new house (well, new to us) everything was peachy-keen. It had a roomy kitchen – perfect for our late-night brownie-making extravaganzas. It had a large living room with green walls – the perfect setting for our many horror-movie nights. And, best of all, it had a master bedroom with dimmed lights and thick, burgundy curtains – perfect for... well, you get the idea.

It was perfect for our quaint little newlywed life.

Perfect until the knocking.

And the whispers in the middle of the night.

The shadows glimpsed out of the corners of our eyes.

When Dave and I both started having the same dream about a sad little girl in a blue-and-white-checkered dress, we decided it was time to call a professional.

Dave believes in ghosts with the conviction of a thousand men. Me, I keep an open mind. I'm willing to believe almost anything. Call a medium? Sure, why not!

Neither of us had ever contacted a medium before. It seemed a little strange, after all. How do you even find one? We assumed you couldn't just look for one in the

why it's so playful. Seems to be a little girl who doesn't understand the boundaries between life and death. It looks like she was murdered, which is..."

He stopped there. Mostly because Dave punched him so hard he dropped to the ground like a sack of rice. He went on punching him for a while as I picked the kid up and set him gently down on the couch.

Dave grabbed one of the ugly throw pillows his mom had bought us and held it down over the bastard's head. He's never really smothered someone so he was a little awkward with it but he held on long enough that I think he probably got the job done. We threw the body in the basement and decided to deal with it later.

It was a few hours before the boy woke up. He looked at us with big doe eyes.

"Where is he?"

"Gone," I answered.

He nodded. "That's good."

"Yeah."

Dave smiled at him. "You want some spaghetti?"

For the first time, I saw the kid smile. And it was gorgeous and precious and perfect. I fell in love all at once. "Yeah! It's my favorite!"

So, long story short, we adopted a nine-year-old kid and decided to name him Matthew. Anyway, does anyone have advice on how to get rid of a dead body?

CHAPTER 14.

ANNIE, QUEEN OF THE PIGS

My grandmother is the sweetest woman you're ever likely to meet. She's one of those women who spoils her grandkids rotten. Her whole life is a monument to human kindness: baking bread for the entire neighborhood on a whim, volunteering at the local nursing home, delivering food for those who can't leave their homes... she's the saint of our little town, as anybody could tell you.

But now my grandmother is dying... old age does that to people, or so I've been told. They say she'll go any day now. I've been staying with her in the hospital, my father, mother, brother, sister, and I keeping constant vigil. Her husband passed years before, as did her own brothers and sisters, and she seems at peace with the fact that she will meet them again soon.

There was, however, one incident a few days ago. There was a single break in the continuity of my grandmother, a change in her life's history that I can't get out of my mind.

Until that morning, she had told me very little about her own life, her own family. What she had told me started with her leaving the old farmhouse to attend nursing school. Everything before that was simply a mystery... until now.

This is the account she gave me, transcribed as well as my memory would allow. I intend to burn these papers when I'm done, but for now, I simply have to write down what I've been told. Whether that will make it less real or more, it is sure to be more bearable than it is now.

———————

I grew up in a dilapidated farmhouse way out in Minnesota, stranded out in the countryside. There were eight of us kids, myself included. We may not have had the most money, but we were far from poor. We were always happy, always playing together, always having fun. What more could you ask for?

Of course, we also managed to get into heaps of trouble. That's what farm kids used to do, you know. We'd see just how far we could push mom and dad until they got angry, or worse, disappointed. We were swatted once or twice, of course. Once was for using the chicken eggs to make mud pies... your great grandmother was none too pleased with that development. Clem got it once for greasing the toilet seat before your great great grandma went out to the outhouse... she never came back to our house again, I'll tell you that much.

Most of the trouble we got into, though, wasn't dangerous – smoking corn silk, for example, wasn't bad for anything but our own stomachs. Once in a while, however, we would do something really, very stupid. And if we were lucky, nothing bad happened.

But sometimes, something did.

I was about twelve years old at the time, so I was young, but old enough to know better. My sister, Greta, was eleven. She and I were given the task of watching our youngest sister, Annie.

Annie was four years old at the time and a regular little terror. She was a brat if I ever saw one, constantly screaming and running around like a little beast. Oh, sure, I loved her, only I didn't know it yet. All I knew was that she was my most annoying little sister, and I hated having to look after her: as the oldest girl, I always had to look after the babies.

That morning, Greta and I took Annie outside to play. It was early summer, so it wasn't too hot. Plus, it would give Annie a chance to run around and scream outside for a change. I was praying that she'd tire herself out so that that afternoon we could have some peace and quiet for once.

Of course, that didn't happen.

Annie was doing her best to terrorize Greta and I. She was pulling my hair and kicking dirt at Greta. She screamed her rotten little head off. And nothing Greta and I did seemed to calm her down. We tried making her hollyhock dolls. We made flower crowns. We alternately cooed lullabies and scolded. But nothing work. She just kept on being the little brat she was.

Finally, I just lost my temper. I just couldn't take it any more. Annie thought she was special, just because she was the youngest. She thought she could get away with everything. Well, I wasn't having it. I decided that it was up to me to teach her a lesson.

"Greta, take Annie," I said. My voice was like ice. There was no life, no feeling to it. There was only this cold anger. Greta must have sensed it because she did what I

CHAPTER 15.

HOMEMADE PUMPKIN PIE

Fall had descended upon the little town of Maplewood, and everything was dying. The leaves fell from the trees like the loose strands of a cancer victim's hair. The dead, dry grass rattled in the wind, like brittle bones in the crumbling bodies of the forgotten. Orange and red cloaked the fields like mourning clothes and a sickly sweet smell filled the air as flowers decayed in the little town's well-kept gardens.

Everything was dying. It was impossible to miss the signs. But this year, as with every year, people did the best they could.

They shut their eyes to the growing cold by claiming the delights of sipping hot cocoa next to the fireplace. They carved pumpkins to avoid watching them rot in the fields, absentmindedly choosing destruction over the slow-moving horror of inevitability. They plastered dancing turkeys and cartoon trees with smiles and watchful eyes, as though such sentinels would protect them from the truth.

Still, in the end, they felt it. They felt it deep in their bones the way you feel the icy breath of an oncoming snowstorm.

Although the melancholy of this grim reminder of mortality had spread throughout the township, the children were blissfully unaware of its implications. They still believed in their own impervious nature, their immortality. So as the adults turned their minds towards the eventuality of winter, the children prepared for Halloween with the conviction that that long-sought day would never come, never end, and never pass away in fragmented memory.

All stories are interwoven, and there exists no true beginnings or endings. But if this story had to choose a point from which to begin its narration, it would fall on a Friday just one week prior to Halloween. The scene must open upon two young boys, about twelve years old, tramping through Maplewood's small Catholic cemetery, the old caretaker shuffling off in the distance, raking leaves from the newer graves as the boys shift within the shadows of the trees.

It was in this place that the lingering pulse of death, its melody and memory, could best be captured. The two boys had been drawn in by that ambiance, sojourners in a land as yet unknown to them, and at that moment, all that mattered was that the light sweetness of death had attracted the living from out their own bitterness.

In the distance, a familiar old stone sat embedded in the earth, watching the world live and die. Watching the boys in their argument.

"I'm telling you, it's true! My older brother told me he had a friend whose cousin did it."

"Unbaptized babies? That's not fair, it's not their fault they weren't baptized."

"Well, who cares about that anyway? We're not looking for any babies. We're looking for the witch."

"Tommy, you don't seriously believe in all that, do you?"

"She's out here." Tommy's face was grim and determined, unmoving as granite.

The following half hour was a wild goose chase, Andy following as Tommy zig-zagged through trees and rocks, searching for an inconspicuous little mound of earth. Andy trailed behind in annoyed silence, hoping that Tommy would tire himself out so that they could go to his house and play videogames. Tommy had the best games because his mom spoiled him rotten. Perks of being the youngest, Andy grumbled.

"It's here, it's here!!"

Andy was startled out of his reverie, and bounded up to Tommy's side, momentarily caught up in the excitement of an old legend. Tommy, for his part, stared down at the unsettled earth with triumph, yet remained at a respectful distance.

Andy stared down at Tommy's trophy. The disturbed dirt formed an oval about six feet long and four feet wide. No grass surrounded the mound. It was as though this earth had been long dead. The north end of the supposed grave had a smooth stone about a foot long, completely unmarked and indistinct.

"Are you kidding? This is it?"

Tommy stared at the nothingness as though it meant something.

"There's no way this is her grave."

"Of course it is. Don't you see the dirt? No grass grows here 'cause she was so evil."

"Stupid, the dirt looks like it was just dug up. If she was buried a hundred years ago, why does it look so fresh?"

"Well, then what do you make of the rock that just-so-happens to be at the head of the grave?"

"Well, what the hell am I *supposed* to make of a stupid rock?"

Tommy was losing his patience. "Look, all the older kids come out to see if the legend is real and Danny told me his friend's cousin actually died 'cause of it."

This was met with eye rolls and a frustrated sigh.

Everyone knew the legend about the Witch of Maplewood. No one could tell you anything about the witch herself: her story had been long forgotten, not that it mattered, anyway. What was important was the mystery behind her grave.

It was said that if you stood on the witch's grave and said your own name three times, the witch would begin to haunt you. After three days' time she'd kill you. The details of the deaths varied based on who you asked. The younger kids usually said it was a knife to the heart but the older kids gave much more graphic, rewarding descriptions, usually involving evisceration and beheadings. The only way to save yourself was to bring an apple to the witch's resting place at midnight and leave it at the foot of the grave. That was supposed to appease her and send her packing back into the depths of Hell.

The nature of this urban legend prompted Andy's next inquiry.

"Ok, then, how did he die?"

"What do you mean, how did he die?"

"You got rocks in your ears or somethin'? How did the witch kill him? Surely Danny must have told you *that*."

Tommy sniffed in disgust, an action that Andy deemed completely unnecessary. "You don't ask that kinda stuff about a person's death, you moron."

As the bickering and teasing continued, a murder of crows gathered in the trees, quietly watching the invasion of their sacred territory with vengeful eyes.

The crows watched on as Andy suddenly fell silent.

"Hey, what's up with you?" Tommy asked.

"Tommy...we haven't thought up our Halloween prank yet, have we?"

"You got something?"

"Yeah...something that will make us legends."

With that, the boys began to plot and scheme in the graveyard, kept under the silent dominion of the old stone.

━━━━━━━━

A small yellow house with white trim sat in the center of Maplewood, quietly situated among the sleepy residences that made up the little town. Nondescript though it was, it held its own secrets and stories, vignettes of human life undisclosed to the prying eyes of the outside world. The drama that unfolded within the confines of its paneled doors could rival the romances of Shakespeare, the horrors of Stoker, the tragedies of Poe. To some, a prison. To others, a refuge. To all, a home.

Inside the small yellow house was an equally small woman, standing at the kitchen counter amidst a chaos of baking ingredients. This woman, Anita Davis, had a story quite unique among the others' of the town, yet it is a common story all the same.

Growing up she was known as Anita Stanton, a little girl with a big heart and large, curious eyes to match. It was the eyes that first caused people concern. Being as big as they were, they could not hide their inquisitiveness, intelligence, expressiveness.

At age three she read her first book. Her parents were delighted. They carefully hid their apprehension. By age nine she was devouring Faulkner, Fitzgerald, and Brontè. Her parents forced her into sports. In middle school she began to excel in mathematics and the sciences. Her parents urged her to get out of the house more, have some fun for God's sake, you're only young once. Her ambition grew with her parents' fears.

All the townsfolk saw what was happening. Though it was something that could never be expressed in open, explicit terms, it was an undercurrent of feeling that was equally potent: she was too smart for the town. Maplewood had no need of a girl that read Whitman or calculated complicated formulas.

It was a relief to everyone when she got her first boyfriend at seventeen. It was even more comforting when her fate was sealed six months after when she became pregnant. For a small-town girl like her, there was no abortion, no adoption, no question of abandoning her responsibilities as a woman. She would bear the child. And with its life came the death of all she had once dreamed.

So the townsfolk were consoled. Anita became the housewife to Anthony Davis and bore two sons, Danny and Tommy. She became all she was meant to be. By all accounts, she had succeeded.

And yet sometimes you could catch her staring longingly out that kitchen window that she had spent so much of her life enclosed behind. In her eyes was a world of forgotten hopes and dreams, those things she had buried inside her heart until they had calcified into stone. Those big eyes were misted over as though covered in cataracts as she watched an unknown world pass her by.

Such was live for Anita Davis.

It was, in fact, at just such a moment that Tommy and Andy traipsed through the front door, laughing and chattering. The words dribbled out of her mouth without much thought.

"Oh, good, Tommy, you're home. Where were you after school? It's almost an hour since classes ended."

Tommy and Andy told their oft-rehearsed lie: "Oh, we were just at the convenience store, having a few snacks and hanging out with some of the other boys in school." They couldn't possibly explain the strange draw of the cemetery at this time of year. It was as though it held a dark, strange secret that it was inviting them to unlock.

"Mmm." His mother continued to look out the window. Tommy became nervous and Andy remained silent. Tommy was old enough now to realize the oddity of his own mother and to be embarrassed by her. He cleared his throat to catch her attention.

All at once her eyes widened and she wrenched them from the window. "Oh, you brought Andy with you! Have a seat, I'll fix you boys a snack."

A snack even though they had just told her they'd eaten at the convenience store. That's how they knew she hadn't heard what they'd said. It wasn't a matter of her choosing not to listen. It was as though she was trapped somewhere beyond their voices' reach.

But such matters did not concern them. They had more important business that demanded their attention.

"Hey, mom, I think dad wanted to see you, he's working out in the shed."

Another shameless lie from the cracked lips of adolescence.

"Mm, I'll be back in a moment then. Could you boys watch the kitchen while I'm out? I've some pies baking in the oven."

Indeed there were pies in the oven, with more yet to be made. Pumpkin pies, to be exact.

Anita Davis had one womanly trick that had helped make her more palatable to the town even during her dangerous ambitious phase. She could bake. Her pies were heavenly, her cakes were divine, and her cookies were to die for. Each year she was called upon for town-wide bake sales and parties. This, at least, kept her busy year-round.

And this month's Fall Festival called for the baking of pumpkin pie.

This Tommy and Andy knew. They approached the kitchen counter, staring not at the pies already baking in the oven, but at the pumpkin filling that sat in a giant bowl next to four waiting pie crusts.

The plan was truly genius.

For generations, the town's children had lived in fear of the witch's grave. The only way to pass from childhood to adulthood was to overcome this fear and impose it on the children that followed. In this way, the legend existed in the minds of all the townspeople.

So it would be fair to say that the horror of this prank as well as its ingenuity would be lost on no one.

The premise was simple enough. Steal a few handfuls of dirt from the witch's grave and mix it into the pumpkin pie filling. They would sell well at Maplewood's Fall Festival, as Mrs. Davis's pies always did, so they could be sure that a large portion of the town would eat the dirt-infused baked goods. The day of Halloween, they would reveal to their classmates their infamous crime. The horror of unwittingly consuming the earth of their very nightmares would be enough to shock them into a state of panic without, of course, actually hurting anyone. Soon the rumor would spread through the town and the boys would become famous. They would be untouchable, as no one could definitively prove their involvement. The evidence would be gone, ingested by those most inflamed by the rumor. In this way they would become a part of the very legend that they emulated.

The plan really was genius, in all aspects but careful consideration of the consequences.

The boys didn't consider what would happen if Tommy's mother noticed the black flecks in the filling. They didn't consider that their confession would be enough proof to lead to serious backlash. They didn't consider the ensuing panic might be uncontrollable and people might get hurt.

They didn't consider that something might go wrong.

Because, of course, nothing would go wrong. That was what was so brilliant. A perfectly executed plan would yield perfect results.

So the boys stood in front of the bowl, a handful of dirt pulled from the side pocket of Andy's backpack.

"Andy, I don't think this is a good idea."

"What, are you gonna wuss out on me now?"

"What if the witch curses everyone in town?"

"Don't be stupid. Even if there is a witch, she only curses the people who stand on her grave and say her name three times. It's not like the actual dirt is gonna hurt anyone. It'll just give people a scare, that's all. That's what Halloween's about, anyway, isn't it?"

With that, Andy concluded by pouring a good portion of the dirt into the pie filling. Enough so that each person who ate the pie would get a healthy serving while the black flakes remained hidden in the depths of the thick, rich orange of the pumpkin.

"There, now you stir it in. Hurry up, before your mom gets back!"

Tommy, adrenaline pumping through his veins at the thought of what his mother might do if she caught him at his little prank, pulled the old wooden spoon through the mixture and watched the black dirt disappear. The boys then rushed back to their seats, returning to their snack as though their very lives depending on its consumption.

Anita returned not a moment later.

"Your dad said he didn't need anything, Tommy."

"Oh, really?" His heart beat like a train speeding down rusted tracks. "Maybe I heard him wrong. Sorry, mom."

"It's alright, I needed a break from all this baking, anyway. You two boys go and have fun, but mind that Andy gets home for supper so his mom doesn't worry."

"Yes, mom."

As they descended into the basement, the realm of video games and pizza rolls, Tommy looked back at his mother and felt a pang of unbearable guilt. All the work that she had put in to this Fall Festival and he had ruined it. What would the adults do to his mother if they discovered the transgression? Another nasty thought he hadn't considered.

He was on the verge of spilling everything when Andy called him from the basement.

"Hey, hurry up, I wanna play that new game!"

He tore his gaze away and trotted down the stairs, his guilt melting like snow.

So their work was completed.

———

Maplewood's Fall Festival occurred that Sunday. Everything went off without a hitch, splendid as usual. Six of Anita's pies were sold, with two cut into pieces and sold by the slice for hungry wanderers. Tommy and Andy ran around the festival, peering into the craft fair and trying the various goodies and candies that the vendors offered. They occasionally returned to Mrs. Davis's pie stand to see how the sales were coming along. The evident popularity of her pies assured the boys of their prank's success. Once they were thus reassured, they headed back to Tommy's house for the afternoon. Late that night, Andy returned to his house and for both of them the night was passed in uneventful silence.

Cue next morning. Andy sat munching his cereal at the breakfast table. Sarah was chatting excitedly about some school activity they were having for Halloween. Andy's mother busied herself around the kitchen, responding to Sarah's blather with the appropriate responses of, "mhm" and, "my, isn't that nice." Andy's father walked back in from retrieving the morning paper, flipping through it dutifully.

Andy was just placing his bowl in the sink and grabbing his backpack when his father exclaimed, "well, isn't that a damned shame!"

"Dear, the children…"

"Uuh, a darned shame."

Amanda Hayes, Andy and Sarah's mother, was perhaps the only woman in town who dared talk back to her husband. James Hayes had always been a quiet, easy-going type and preferred to let his wife rule over the household in whatever way she so pleased. The difference between Andy and Tommy's households made it even stranger that Anita and Amanda were such good friends.

"What happened, dear?"

"You remember Mrs. Thompson, our old Sunday school teacher?"

A crotchety old woman whose heart was always in the right place despite her strict nature. "Sure, I just saw her on Sunday at the Fall Festival. Why?"

"Looks like she passed away last night."

Amanda stared at her husband with a look of abject shock. Although she had scared her when she was a child, Amanda had a special place in heart for Mrs. Thompson now that she had grown up. She was a fixture in her life, an immoveable constant. Having always existed since her earliest childhood, Amanda had simply assumed Mrs. Thompson would always be a part of the town. "What? What happened?"

"They're not sure yet. It looks like a heart attack. Isn't that just terrible. What a wonderful old lady."

"Bless her soul. She's finally joined her husband in Heaven." Although Amanda said this, she knew that Mrs. Thompson had been the first to pour the champagne after her dictator of a husband died in that car crash in '85.

Andy had been listening to this exchange with apprehension. He stared on at his mother and father until Sarah pulled at his coat sleeve.

"Come on, Andy, we're going to be late!"

"Oh, right, sorry, Sarah."

They set out for school. Andy pretended to take an interest in Sarah's prattle, and she joyfully accepted his feigned interest as she skipped next to Andy's side. He dropped her off at the elementary schoolyard and continued down the street to the imposing brick building that housed the middle school and high school.

Tommy was already waiting for him in the hallway, his face paler than usual. He must have heard. Andy cursed to himself. Tommy was a bit sensitive and was sure to blow this out of proportion.

"You heard, huh?"

"Andy, mom said that Mrs. Thompson was one of the ladies who bought pie at the fair yesterday. You don't suppose..."

"Can it, you moron. Pie with a little dirt in it is not going to kill anyone. She was an old hag and dropped dead from a heart attack. It happens. Come on, let's go or we'll be late for class."

And so the matter dropped, but Tommy continued to wear a distressed look on his face for the rest of the day.

———————

The next death came that night. A Mr. Coleman had been walking in the park when his breathing began to slow. He fell to the ground, choking on air while his granddaughter, a 17-year-old high school student he affectionately called Suzie Q, screamed for help.

Although the cemetery caretaker happened upon the scene and called 911, it was already too late. By the time the sleepy town awoke and sent its best men, Mr. Coleman had stopped breathing and Suzie was wailing by his side, trying to administer CPR without the proper knowledge to do so. He was pronounced dead at the hospital with Suzie Q in a room a few doors down, being sedated so her parents could come pick her up.

Tommy began to shake when the news arrived at his house. Word spreads quickly in a small town, and Maplewood was no exception. Anita stared in disbelief as Anthony relayed to her the details of the death gleaned from conversations with the neighbors.

"That's awful! Mr. Coleman was such a sweetie. You know his granddaughter doted on him so much, the poor dear. Come to think of it, I think I sold a pie to his wife. She was going to surprise him with it, apparently pumpkin was his favorite. Don't you think it's a bit odd?"

Tommy didn't sleep that night. In his heart was infinite remorse and a growing fear that was quickly turning into terror. What had they done? Nothing, he hoped.

But he began to fear that hope was in vain.

Danny sat on his bed, headphones in and fingers whirling on his phone's keyboard, desperately trying to woo Emily Ryers into sending him a shirtless picture. He'd just used his best line on her (do you believe in love at first sight, or do you want to take a look at me one more time?) when Tommy slunk into the room, his face ashen and his hands shaking.

"Danny, I gotta talk to you."

A quick evaluation on Danny's part put him on the defensive. Danny had been with Tommy from the moment he was born, changing his diaper, pulling his hair, and scaring him senseless in the small hours of the morning, prompting Anita to move Tommy to his own room. Seeing Tommy so distraught led Danny to one conclusion: he was NOT going to be blamed for this.

"Sure, Tommy, what's up?" *Play it cool, be nice for once, maybe you can fix whatever it is you fucked up,* his brain stuttered.

"I wanna ask you a question about the witch's grave."

Fuck. Of course it was his fault. Danny silently cursed Tommy out: wasn't he a little too old to believe in this bullshit? (Never mind the fact that Danny slept with a nightlight until he was well past thirteen.)

"Ok, yeah, sure, what's up?"

"Well... how does the witch kill people?"

Danny was faced with a decision of the utmost importance. He had three options. The most fun – and dangerous – option would be to give the most grisly death account he could, then chase Tommy around the house until he cried. But when he thought about the beating in store from his father, he ruled against it. Option two: he could tell Tommy that it was all bullshit. However, if he did that, he couldn't torture Tommy with the story in the future, and he wasn't quite ready to give up that privilege. Final choice: he could play it smooth and come up with a relatively non-threatening death scene so Tommy wouldn't have nightmares and he wouldn't get into trouble.

Option three it was.

"Oh, they just sorta drop dead, you know? Looks like a heart attack or something. Not a bad way to go, really."

At this, Tommy's face turned roughly the color of a blank sheet of paper and his whole body shuddered. "Oh." Just that syllable, then he turned on his heel and left the room.

"Shit," Danny muttered, considering whether or not to go after them. But just then, a picture message arrived from Emily, and all thoughts of his dorky little brother were lost.

———

No more deaths were reported that night. The peace continued through all of Tuesday. Andy began to relax. Although Mr. Coleman's death had shaken him, he realized that his fears were impossibly fantastic to be real. Although Tommy was not so easily assuaged, he began to relax at least a little. The boys congregated at the cemetery once more to discuss their prank.

"Andy, we should never have done it."

"Chill, Tommy, it's a joke. Look, two people are dead, sure, but that ain't got nothing to do with us. My dad was talkin' about it last night. When the weather gets cold, he said, old people start dropping off like flies. It's just a part of life. Don't read so much into it."

Tommy's eyes began to fill with tears, much to Andy's discomfort.

"But, Andy, I talked to Tommy about the grave again and he said…"

"Hey, come on, Tommy, enough of that grave shit, don't go getting upset. Hey, how about we go back to my place and watch some scary movies? We can do it in the basement, mom won't know. C'mon, it'll be fun!"

Tommy brushed the tears aside impatiently. "Nah, I can't today. Maybe tomorrow, ok?"

With that the boys left the graveyard, peeling themselves away from the calming aura of the cemetery with its lush grass, quiet atmosphere, and old stone tucked away in the corner. As they turned towards their homes, they felt separated in more ways than one.

Andy got home and his heart stopped.

"Hey, hun, where ya' been? Sarah just finished up having some of Mrs. Davis's world-famous pumpkin pie! I can get you a slice if you want one."

Andy stared endlessly at the empty plate in front of Sarah, clean save for a few small crumbs. "Uh... no thanks, that's ok, I think I'm going to go to my room for a bit." He retreated upstairs, his heart racing.

The deaths had nothing to do with the pie, he reminded himself. It was a coincidence, nothing more than that. His heart beat rapidly.

It would be fine. It would be fine.

Andy found himself back in the cemetery. It was full dark without even the moon to illuminate his path. He was stumbling forward as though blind. He looked up to the sky, seeing only the vague shapes of thunderous black clouds. Everything was silent, so utterly silent.

He looked down at his hand. He was holding a shiny, red apple.

When he looked back up, he was in the woods. But it was a part of the woods he didn't recognize. He whirled around, looking for the meticulously placed gray stones of the cemetery, but none were in sight. He ran aimlessly through the trees, never getting far from his starting point.

Then, suddenly, a clock struck in the distance, one lonely toll. An icy fear spread over his heart as he heard rustling behind him.

"Too late, too late, you're all too late!"

He turned back as a dry cackling filled his ears. His eyes tried to take it all in: a gray tattered dress, coal black eyes, rotting skin...

She flew at him.

A few hours later Andy awoke to a commotion coming from the living room.

Through blurring eyes he stared at the clock. Six o'clock, proclaimed the glowing green numbers. He must have fallen asleep waiting for dinner. As the fog in his head lifted he heard his mother and father shouting downstairs. Andy felt a sense of dread creeping into his chest, but he couldn't remember what might be causing it. He rushed downstairs, stumbling and reeling along the way, trying to regain his footing in the real world.

"James, call an ambulance!"

"It will take too long, we better just take her to the hospital. Get her into the car, I'll get Andy."

Just then James saw Andy standing on the stair landing, shock spreading over his features.

There lay Sarah, motionless on the ground. Her breathing was coming in spurts when it came at all. Her eyes were glazed and tears streamed down her face. Andy leaned over the railing and vomited.

James paid no attention to the mess on the floor. "Andy, I need you to stay calm. Get in the front seat, we're taking Sarah to the hospital."

That car ride was the single most painful moment of Andy's life. His father drove maniacally, swerving in and out of what little traffic existed on the quiet interstate. Although it usually took about twenty minutes to reach the hospital, his father got there in ten.

Amanda, meanwhile, was holding Sarah in the backseat, crooning to her and begging her to stay awake. Each of Sarah's breaths was labored and slow. They grew weaker by the minute. Amanda was losing her wits, crying and shouting. James tried in vain to console her as he ran the last stop sign on the way to the hospital.

Andy stared off into the darkness as he felt his world collapsing in on itself.

———————

"What the hell's wrong with her?"

"I don't know, there's nothing obstructing the airway!"

"Her heartbeat isn't irregular, it couldn't have been a heart attack..."

"Dammit, we have to do something!"

"Let's get a breathing tube in her?"

"There's no time!"

Beep... Beep... Beeeeeeeeeeep.

Time of death, 6:30 PM.

———————

Tommy's dread had been building all afternoon... to what end, he couldn't yet divine. But it felt as though something awful was just around the corner. It was like in a horror movie when the audience knows the serial killer is just behind the door that the big-breasted blonde was about to carelessly yank open...

It broke when his mother got the phone call.

"Davis residence. Oh, hi, James, if you're looking for Tony... What? Slow down, what happened? Oh... oh my god. Okay, I'll be right over. Should I bring... Ok, ok. I'll be there soon."

Tommy stared at his mother's ashen face. She stared for a moment at the phone, as though unsure as to how to proceed. Finally, she turned to Tommy with a bravery in her eyes that he'd never seen before.

"Tommy, I want you to listen carefully. There's been an accident and Andy's little sister was hurt. I know this is hard for you, but we need to go to the hospital. Andy's waiting there for you and his mother needs me. Can you do this with me, Tommy?"

Tommy was momentarily swept away from this nightmare by the determination in his mother's voice. Her face was calm and poised. He was awed by the magnitude of her presence. It was as though a part of her had been long asleep until she got that phone call.

He was subdued. "I can do it," he muttered weakly. He held on desperately to his reason.

"Good. Let's get in the car."

It was approximately 6:45 when Tommy and Anita arrived at the hospital. By this time, the family had already received the news.

Amanda was screaming expletives at the doctor, fighting for his throat while James held her back, trying to coax her into calming down. As they struggled, the doctor ordered his assistant to fetch a sedative, not bothering with thorny matters of consent. Andy sat off in one of the waiting room chairs, staring in silence.

Out of this little scene of horrors, the worst sight was Andy's face. It was sheet white and utterly expressionless, as though he was the one that had died and not his baby sister. There was nothing in his eyes other than dejection. He looked like a man who had seen the infinity of the universe and understood for the first time the fact of his utter and unforgiving solitude.

As Anita helped James calm Amanda down, Tommy sat gingerly next to Andy.

"What happened?"

Andy was still and silent. He didn't seem to hear a word anyone said. Tommy was about to reiterate his question when Andy's lips finally parted imperceptibly.

"...her."

The sentence sounded little more than a breath of air.

"I can't hear you, Andy."

"We killed her."

Silence. The kind of silence that the world makes as it condemns you.

"What do you mean?"

"You know what I mean."

"She ate it?"

"Yeah."

"You're sure?"

"The witch got her. The witch is real, Tommy, and she got my sister, and it's been more than three days. It's too late, Tommy."

Andy was already gone. Tommy was on his way. The guilt of what they did had weighed on him from the very beginning. Now the guilt was too heavy. He felt cracks forming in the contours of his mind.

"Andy... we gotta tell."

"Yeah."

———

When Tommy tearfully confessed to his mother their awful deed, a rash of emotions shook her all at once. First, blinding rage at the stupidity of the boys. They'd done something as stupid and dangerous as putting dirt in those pies that they knew would be fed to a substantial portion of the town. Hadn't they considered the consequences? What the fuck had been running through their feeble little minds?

Next was confusion. Dirt, although disgusting, wasn't fatal upon ingestion. Although she could not deny the connection, she also couldn't possibly understand it. There was a part of the puzzle missing... but what?

Then it was pure horror. Was it really the pies that had done it? If so, wasn't she partly responsible, as Tommy's mother and as the baker? What would happen to her and her son? She thought with painful guilt of Amanda, lying sedated in the hospital bed, with James next to her, sobbing into his calloused hands.

Finally, a cold shiver ran down her spine as she knew what she had to do.

"Andy, get your father. We're going to the police."

"Okay, kid. You said you took the dirt from some "witch's grave," right? Well, where is it?"

"It's out in the woods, where they used to bury the bad people."

"Kid, there's no one buried out there. This cemetery isn't near old enough to be sectioned off like that. Are you sure the dirt you took was from a grave?"

"I'm positive. It really was!"

"Well, alright, take us to it, then."

Floyd Sanderson had been the caretaker of the Maplewood Catholic Cemetery for over forty years. In a way, he was not so different from Anita Davis. He was born in this town, he had lived all his life in this town, and he would most likely die in this town. He had watched the world change while Maplewood stayed eternally the same.

And, like Anita, he had unrealized ambitions.

From birth, he was destined to be the cemetery caretaker, like his father and grandfather before him. But from early childhood he knew that what he really wanted was to be a mortician.

He was fascinated with the dead, had been ever since he had watched his own mother, Tess, die slowly from tuberculosis, her face taking on the pallor of death as her own throat betrayed her to suffocation. In reality, she was dead long before her heart stopped beating. She lay underneath an old stone in a far corner of the little cemetery, sleeping peacefully in a way she couldn't during the last few months of her life.

After witnessing her demise, Floyd became entranced by the beauty of death. The end of suffering, the quieting of the restless mind, the return of peace. To him, death was a miracle far superior to the so-called gift of life.

At first, it was animals. He had inherited the caretaker position at twenty years old when his father took a drunken spill into the nearby ravine and drowned. The job wasn't so hard and he had a lot of free time. Occasionally an animal would wander into the cemetery, a skunk or a cat or a dog. These times were very special for Floyd.

It took him years to find the proper blend of chemicals to preserve the bodies. He knew that morticians used formaldehyde, but what else went into the mix? Searching for the answer in the miniscule town library proved useless and he had to research via the process of elimination, enduring dozens of bloated, misshapen bodies in the process. Those ugly imperfections he burned.

After years of trial and error he finally stumbled upon a suitable mix of chemicals, mostly based on formaldehyde with a few other solutions found in unmarked bottles in his father's workshop.

This was when the real experiments began.

The first was a 20-year-old college student from about thirty miles over. Her first name was Annabelle, but he never learned her last. She came out of a club, drunk and stumbling, alone and confused. He hauled her home without much of a struggle and strapped her to a table.

She had to look perfect. He drained her blood to keep from marring the sanctity of her body. Like anyone else, he had principles.

He worked with his crude embalming fluid, dollar store makeup, and an old dress of his mother's, transforming the drunken slut into an immaculate picture of innocence and beauty.

He kept her in his home for a week before burying her in the woods.

Over the years there were others. Alice Manchester, who was hitchhiking across the country when Floyd pulled over. Isabel Hernandez, whose thick black hair had entranced Floyd in the back alley behind a nightclub. Mary Cunningham, the youngest of his victims, only twelve year old when he dolled up her hair and shoved her into the ground.

The most recent body was no one special, another drunk girl he picked up from the same bar that Annabelle had stumbled out of twenty years ago. She was in such a state that she didn't even remember her own name, but that was just perfect for Floyd. He'd done a really magnificent job on this one. He had the perfect bubblegum pink lipstick to match the natural blonde of her hair and the dark blush gave her face a rosy glow. He picked a prime spot to bury her, just beyond the confines of the cemetery in a little clearing where the sun shone brightest in the summer.

It was to this shallow grave that Tommy led the police.

Although Floyd was unduly proud of his home-style embalming fluid, the plain truth of the matter was that it didn't work particularly well. After a week or so the body deteriorated quite rapidly. Although Annabelle had only been buried a little over a month before, her body had collapsed in on itself and was now unrecognizable. A terrible stench filled the air, a stench tainted with a strong, chemical smell.

Officer Keillor, the man that Tommy had led to the witch's grave, was a man of more than a few years. Having previously been on the force in New York City, he had moved to Maplewood to endure his career quietly and peacefully until he could retire. His years of experience and a quick assessment of the body and its smell led him to a conclusion that months of testing would ultimately indicate to be true.

"This dirt is soaked in formaldehyde. When her body started rotting and her veins collapsed, the formaldehyde exited her body and got into the ground. I'm guessing those folks in town died from formaldehyde poisoning."

Andy was standing off at a distance, guarded tensely by his father. When Andy heard the news, he began to shake uncontrollably.

"I poisoned Sarah."

James did not reply. He didn't have the heart to console his son. Although he would never admit it to a living soul, he had hardened towards Andy. To him, Andy had killed his youngest daughter.

"I poisoned Sarah."

Anita left Tommy's side as the rookie of the police department watched him carefully. She took Andy by the shoulders.

"Get ahold of yourself, Andy. It's not your fault. You need to calm down."

I would like to say that when Andy's mind snapped he broke down into dramatic hysterics, screaming at the sky and cursing the face of God. I'd like to say that with his insanity came a heart-rending display of emotion that brought tears to the eyes of everyone present.

I would like to, but I would be lying.

Andy collapsed onto the ground, senseless and motionless. Already he had ceased to exist.

He would never utter another word.

Some people believe that tragedies, especially those of the unique and horrific breed, are never forgotten in small towns, branded onto the memory of those whose lives have been otherwise uneventful and monotone.

These people underestimate the power of the mind.

Tragedies are forgotten selectively. Anything that betrays the truth behind the pleasant façade of friendly neighborhoods and familiarity is unceremoniously destroyed.

Andy was institutionalized without a word. After a few months, Amanda and James Hayes stopped visiting him, not that he noticed, in his catatonic state. They quietly pretended that he had never existed, hating him in the secret chambers of their hearts. They would never speak his name again. When the townsfolk talked about the Hayes family, as they did, from time to time, they would say what a shame it was that their only child, Sarah, had died so suddenly, and yet no one would be able to put into words exactly what had happened.

Anita Davis tried to remain strong, relying on the reawakening of her own soul that began with that fateful phone call. But the town wore her down. They could not forgive her for what they saw as her part in the ordeal. Amanda refused to speak to her ever again. Anthony grew cold towards her. She drew dark stares when she was shopping at the supermarket. Although she persisted for a few years in this manner, in the end she succumbed to the will of the town as she had once done in the folly of her youth. Her husband found her hanging by a scarf in their bedroom one late fall afternoon. He had her cremated and threw the urn into the landfill at the edge of town. And that was the end of that.

Anthony and Tommy Davis lived grudgingly together until Tommy turned 18, at which point he disappeared from his father's life. The two would never speak again. Despite Danny's attempts to contact Tommy, he remained lost to the family. A few years later, somewhere in the depths of Detroit, Tommy would overdose on heroin, screaming about witches and apples and pie. He must have had a bad trip.

Anthony and Danny would never learn of his fate.

Slowly, Maplewood returned to normal. Those strange deaths were forgotten and life went on. Children grew up, married, and settled down as their parents had done before them. The Maplewood Fall Festival was as spectacular as always. When Floyd Sanderson was sentenced to death by lethal injection, no one even remembered that he had once been one of their own.

Life continued and ended as Maplewood dictated. And through it all sat the little cemetery with its watchful stone, silently holding dominion over all.

ABOUT THE AUTHOR

Rona Vaselaar developed an interest in horror from an early age. Being surrounded by aging cemeteries, urban legends, and a small, one-room library full of horror stories fed her interest in the darker side of human nature. This eventually became the stories you read here. She lives in rural Minnesota and attends school at the University of Notre Dame.

Made in the USA
San Bernardino, CA
25 August 2017